THE
SETTLING
EARTH

A COLLECTION OF
SHORT STORIES BY

REBECCA BURNS

WITH GUEST WRITER

SHELLY DAVIES

ODYSSEY
BOOKS

Published by Odyssey Books in 2014
978-1-922200-16-7

www.odysseybooks.com.au

National Library of Australia
Cataloguing-in-Publication entry

Author: Burns, Rebecca
Title: The Settling Earth / Rebecca Burns
ISBN: 978-1-922200-16-7 (pbk.)
978-1-922200-07-4 (ebook)
Dewey Number: N 823.914

For Isla, for helping to put us back together again,
and for JAM, with thanks for the Spanish balcony

CONTENTS

A Pickled Egg ~ 1

Mr William Sanderson Strikes for Home ~ 11

Miss Swainson's Girl ~ 21

Dottie ~ 29

Port and Oranges ~ 41

Tenderness ~ 53

Dressed for the Funeral ~ 66

Ink and Red Lace ~ 89

The Beast ~ 101

Balance ~ 111

Publishing Credits ~ 119

The Authors ~ 120

A Pickled Egg

Sarah woke to a fierce north wind. She lay in the creaky marital bed, listening to the wind whip about the little wooden house and, watching the pasted wallpaper billow and bulge as warm air wove between the slats, decided to bake a pie. The bed was deep and comfortable—they had taken an extra trip up to Christchurch to fetch the iron frame, William had insisted upon it. He'd stuck out his chin, a jutting corner of stubbornness. Of course, the bed had made it down to the station—somehow it hadn't dared break. As a rare indulgence, William had ordered a feather mattress from Wellington, and it now lay on the frame like a delicate fruit topping on a sponge base. Sarah pondered. Maybe a fruit pie would be too light after William's long trip. Mutton would be more satisfying.

Her grandmother's carriage clock ticked on the dresser and Sarah turned her gaze from the wallpaper to its opal face. She felt a faint pang when she saw it was a quarter past nine in the morning. She had gone to bed early the night before, but these days she felt so tired.

Her limbs and thighs ached as she wriggled beneath the bedspread. Perhaps it's the weather, she reasoned. It had been oppressive recently; the air hung about the house and garden with a stifling heaviness. Yet it was dry, almost unbearably dry, and the heat accompanying the wind felt like blotting paper on the skin, drawing out all moisture. It had turned the dogs crazy—even Bessie, her favourite. The shaggy black-coated animal had lain panting beside her pen and then, in a thrash of foaming energy, had run off, barking and growling. Sarah hadn't seen her for days. And hadn't she changed her own clothes three times yesterday? Finally she'd removed her corset altogether and sat around the house in a white linen underdress. Sarah nodded to herself and stroked her stomach absently. Perhaps a mutton pie could be baked and left to cool. Hans had slaughtered a wether only yesterday. William might like a cold mutton pie, served with a pickled egg.

But were there any eggs left? Sarah frowned and shook her head, trying to clear the fog in her mind. She could almost see the little cupboard in the kitchen where jars of jams and preserves were neatly stacked, but when she tried to focus on the row of pickled eggs, a cloud obscured her view. It was quite maddening. A shapeless grey mass drifted in front of the labels on the jars. In fact, not just in front of the jars. This baggy grey haze seemed to be there all the time these days. Sometimes, if Sarah tried to remember something important William had said—like when he would leave for town or what shirts he needed her to darn—she could see his mouth and lips move, but the grey cloud would obscure his tongue and suck up all the instructions. It seemed malevolent.

But hadn't she pickled a dozen eggs just last week after wrestling them from the defensive hens as they strutted about in the back yard? She could distinctly remember standing by the fence, watching intently for her moment before shooing away the birds (especially that arrogant speckled one who always seemed to know how to frighten her) and braving the pen where warm brown eggs waited for her. She was sure she had bundled them into her apron, deliberately avoiding the baleful gaze of the birds. Well, hadn't she fed them and kept them clean? Hadn't she protected them from rats and hawks that pecked, pecked, pecked the chicks until their soft yellow bodies fell to the earth? Eggs are eggs, she reasoned, and these eggs are my payment. Still, she hadn't looked back at the hens once she'd left their pen, and she was sure they were still cross with her a week later.

But the fact remained that she had collected a dozen eggs. Hadn't she? She remembered the pent up energy balling in her stomach that day when William had gone away again, and Hans had been on the prowl. Remembering, Sarah sat up a little in bed. She recalled that William had risen early and flapped around the bedroom in his nightshirt, muttering about saddling his horse ready for the trip. She had watched him sleepily, sensing that she should get up and make him breakfast—indeed, that William expected her to—but somehow, she just couldn't. Instead, the vivacity that should have gone to her legs gathered at her centre in a tense, tight knot. It gnawed all day, prompting indigestion that would not shift even after drinking a large glass of warm milk. She had been restless and strolled around house, moving from bedroom to parlour, parlour to kitchen, kitchen to scullery. And, when Hans slid into the kitchen, his eyes wandering over her dress and mumbling something unintelligible, Sarah finally burst into movement. She had hurried out of the way, shrugging off Hans's fingers on her arm, and bustled into the yard. She gazed out at the run, spying the white merino sheep grazing on the horizon. The Southern Alps were pale and blue in the distance, and she lifted up her hands, cupping their silhouettes in her palms. She felt a sudden desire to run along the burnished flats in her bare feet, feeling the rough grass push between her toes, running to the bottom of the hills where jagged grey rocks marked the beginning of the trail. Would the rocks be sharp against her skin? Would they cut her if she scrambled up the mountain? Would they tear her clothes to pieces? She stared at the unreadable hills in the distance, feeling a trickle of perspiration prick her skin. Her clothes felt tight on her body.

The squawking of the chickens had brought her back to herself. Biting her bottom lip, she turned towards the bird house. The sudden, unexpected vigour within had to be channelled somewhere. Hans was too dangerous. Safety lay in pickling, baking and churning. The clean satisfaction of domestic toil would be her refuge. Later, bent over a pot of boiling eggs, she could feel her hair dampening at the temples and wondered if this type of work would be enough for her. But then she heard Hans outside, hammering a fence somewhere on the run. With each metallic stroke, Sarah bit down. The labourer's thud became a metronome to her domesticity, and she peeled eggs and pounded dough in time to his beat.

So she *had* pickled eggs. Sarah nodded to herself in bed. But now she was certain she'd eaten them. She felt slightly appalled. *How could I have eaten a dozen pickled eggs in a week?* In her girlhood, before she came out to New Zealand, she had eaten like a bird. Indeed, her father had been proud of his waif-like daughter, positively glowing as he described her fussiness to their neighbours: "She'll only eat toast and blackberry jam," he would say, and the little man would gleam. Of course, he trumpeted her particular diet in order to advertise his ability to buy only the best for her. There were to be no hearty meals of cheap meat and potatoes for her, not his dainty Sarah. Instead she remained pale and svelte, quite the daughter for a coming man like her father.

Only the depression in Europe, throbbing relentlessly across the sea, turned the business sour. No one could afford to buy ornate fireplaces and Sarah's father spent his time worrying over accounts that would not balance. Toast and jam were replaced with King Edward potatoes and cabbage, and Sarah had to eat. And then one day, her father brought home an old school friend to look at the books. William.

Now, after a couple of years in a febrile climate, with mutton and fat loaves to eat, she had become a little brown barrel. *In fact*, she thought, *I look like an egg—plump, portly, matronly. Perhaps if I'd looked this way back home, William might not have wanted me. Then I would still be with my parents, instead of at the end of a three-month journey to the other side of the world.* It was something to ponder all right.

Thinking of William, Sarah supposed he would be cross with her if he knew she was still in bed at this time of the morning. He seemed so impatient with her recently. A quick, eager man with narrow, pincer-like hands and mottled grey skin. His hair had thinned, and wisps stuck out coarsely from behind his ears. He had a gruff voice and a furrowed way of speaking, as though he wanted to swallow his words and speak in regurgitated bursts. In England he had worn crisp white shirts and polished boots. On the day he proposed, he had come to her father smelling of coal tar soap and his face had an odd, scrubbed look. It reminded Sarah now of the dry grass on the run. He had not looked at her as he mumbled his suggestion to her father. She had sat quietly in an armchair, hands folded neatly on her lap, listening slightly incredulously to this faltering shadow of a man as he made his offer. He was set to go to New Zealand, to a sheep run, and he could help the family by taking Sarah with him. Of course, she would have to agree to it, but what with the slump as it was, and them not having much more to sell for food—well, didn't it make sense to accept his offer? William was an honourable man, after all, never married, never been attached to a scandal (not counting a few furtive visits to city prostitutes), and Sarah would do well by him. On and on William's voice droned in that gulping way and his words washed over her. It got so she couldn't remember what he wanted from her father—all she could focus on was that steady, rhythmic tone. By the time William trailed off, his voice becoming fainter, Sarah felt subdued. She was not at all surprised when her father turned to her, resigned and tearful.

But it wasn't all bad, was it? Sarah now reasoned. William had done what he'd promised—he had taken her out to this distant, topsy-turvy land, with its flat yellowing plains and lush green bush, and had carved a home for them. Not "carve", Sarah considered. More "imposed". Their little wooden house seemed to jut out conspicuously on the run. True, it had a veranda and a good sized porch where Sarah could receive rare guests or hold Sunday morning bible classes. William had worked hard to cultivate a small garden, ringed with English ferns. And the kitchen was well equipped for these parts; Sarah could churn her own butter and roast a whole lamb on the range. Their bedroom and parlour were set up nicely, with embroidered cloths adorning the small card table and easy chair, and a porcelain jug stood proudly on the dresser, ready for the morning wash. William had even thought to frame the sepia photographs of Sarah's parents and they rested on a table next to her side of the bed. She could turn and look at them each morning, or even when she felt lonely, and imagine they were with her.

She felt heavy this morning. What comfort could a scratchy garden with dried plants and faded flowers give to a girl longing to see the pretty, ordered villages of home? True, the porch was large and she could take her sewing out there in the evening to catch the last of the orange light. But a heat that Sarah was not used to soldered the air and made her skin smart for the dampness of home. She particularly missed the old trees, the oak and the willow. Away in the distance, she could make out one solitary tree, unusual on these barren plains. It stood stubbornly against the bitter sou-westers and arid breezes from the north. Once, Sarah had walked all the way up there to see it. She had heard the Captain Cookers crashing through the bush to the far side of the run, their snorts rasping and hooves drumming on the ground. A pair of keas made a brief appearance in the hope of food.

It took her a good hour to reach the tree, far longer than she had expected. It was the furthest she had ever walked from the house. There she stood, gazing up at the branches and leaves, enjoying the dark cool beneath its foliage. It didn't seem to be an old tree and Sarah wondered if some unknown person had planted it as a sapling, perhaps hoping that it would grow and break up the repetitive flatness of the run. She reached out and placed a palm against the sandpaper bark, moving her hand over its warm roughness. The feeling reminded her of William, with his bristly grey face. The tree stood silently, except for a faint rustle of leaves, allowing her to caress it in the sunshine. The grass sprouting at its base seemed richer and fuller than the prickly bush of the run. Insects tumbled between the green blades and flies buzzed about, drawn to the easy pickings beneath the branches.

Sarah sat under the tree for that whole afternoon, her back resting comfortably against the trunk. Ants crawled over her boots and dress, but she didn't mind. To be amongst such life, even if it were only the hum and tumble of insects, was calming and much more satisfying than spending the afternoon in a silent, tidy parlour. One ant even found its way inside her boot and she felt it tickle her ankle all the way back to the homestead. She could see the station in the distance—a small wooden block embroidered against a muddled canvas of yellows, browns and greens. Behind the house a brilliant blue lake glittered in the summer sunshine; Sarah knew its glacial waters would be bitterly cold. She looked back at the tree, feeling a strong sense of communion; they were two displaced, transplanted things in an unfamiliar landscape.

The house creaked again and Sarah drew the bed-clothes around her. She glanced at the clock and saw that it was now almost ten. She sighed and reluctantly swung her legs around so they dangled over the side of the bed. She stood up gingerly, catching sight of her profile in the long, cracked mirror fronting the wardrobe. She frowned. Her stomach, never flat these days, was protruding even more. It stuck out stubbornly, nudging the fabric of her nightdress. Leaning over a little, she could see her bellybutton. Maybe I'm bloated from bread, she thought. Yesterday she had eaten a whole loaf, smeared with butter.

That was it. Sarah sighed again and patted her stomach. Then she turned towards the bedroom door and headed for the kitchen.

Mr William Sanderson
Strikes for Home

Some things could no longer be denied. His horse was
lame. For the last three miles, Albert had stumbled over
uneven, blackened grass, his hooves gamely picking out
a line towards the brown dot in the distance. Up ahead,
the homestead stood silent on the plains. A faint light
flickered in an upstairs window: a tell-tale line of smoke
oozed from the chimney stack like sweat beads on
smooth skin. Mr William Sanderson had been mesmer-
ised by the smoke's movement, his aching, travel-worn
thighs relaxing against Albert's flanks.

But now, as Albert tilted awkwardly from side to side,
Sanderson sighed and suddenly became conscious of
the evening air, still and dry. It had drawn an unnoticed, unsightly sheen from the skins of both horse and
rider, and they shone like the faint light in the distance.
Although Sanderson had removed his corduroy jacket
once on the trail and fully out of sight of the town, the
heat on this New Zealand evening was still suffocating.

His riding boots, newly purchased, were now dusty and heavy on his feet. Albert grunted painfully beneath him. With a resigned, bitter glance at the companion riding alongside him, Sanderson reined the horse to a halt and dismounted.

Haimona also stopped, watching with interest as his fellow rider dismounted. The Māori's brown skin seemed clear of sweat, a fact that did not escape Sanderson as he wiped perspiration from his own brow. Perhaps Haimona's insistence in riding with bare arms saved him. His inappropriate garb, though, put Sanderson's teeth on edge. *Thank goodness we are some distance from decent Christchurch company.*

But, if he allowed a moment of honesty, he would have to admit that not all of the company he kept in Christchurch was decent. As the evening breeze whipped through the tussock grass he compared his visit to the bank and that other place. The deep leather seats and mahogany tables of Harding's Bank spoke of studied, respectable luxury—such a contrast to the place of brass headboards and oiled, naked skin. For a second Sanderson was sure he could detect a faint whiff of perfume in the night air. Snug down a side alley away from the main street and Harding's Bank, Miss Swainson's boarding house was a velvety secret, and her girls had been welcoming and waiting.

The muscles in Sanderson's thighs tightened again. *Calm yourself man*, he thought sternly. *In a couple of weeks I can make my excuses and justify another trip into town. The bank will probably want to see the station's accounts anyway.* And he told himself that, in the meantime, the station and husbandly duties would distract him. But only just. He ducked down to stare at Albert's leg.

"Go lame, eh?" Haimona said suddenly, his quiet low voice carrying in the stillness. A faint blue line creased in his chin as he spoke and he reached out to caress his own horse. "We ask too much of our beasts, Mr Sanderson."

He supposed a gentleman would make conversation, even with a native, but Mr William Sanderson felt in no mood to talk to this unwelcome interloper. He crouched closer to his horse resentfully. He hadn't asked Haimona to join him: circumstances beyond his control had forced them into companionship. And now he was expected to give the Māori shelter overnight on the station, maybe for a few days! Haimona had been quite firm about that. Sanderson gave a little shake of his head, marvelling at the unfairness of it all. He supposed some tribal resistance lay at the root of these unreasonable demands. Why couldn't these natives see this was no longer their country? Why their insufferable rejection of English values and their determination to undermine the colonists' attempts to civilise them? It would have been far better if Haimona had stayed with his people in the north, instead of coming south to barter with farmers and merchants. Haimona should have understood that an Englishman dealt with a Māori only out of necessity. Blast it! Sanderson slapped Albert's flesh sharply, causing the horse to jump in pain. Why did Haimona have to be at Miss Swainson's yesterday?

Then Haimona appeared at his side. Standing up, Sanderson jumped to find the Māori so close to him; Haimona had slid without a sound from his own saddle. He was now working his fingers into a leather pouch tied around his neck, one hand resting on Albert's side. Sanderson stood back. "Please do not do that, Mr Haimona," he said. "You startled me. And kindly remove your hand from my horse."

Haimona's eyes narrowed into brown lines, but he brought his hand back to his side. Slowly, with the other, he drew a small glass vial from the pouch. He held it out towards Sanderson. "For the horse. Rub this on. It will help."

Sanderson eyed the bottle with distaste. A clear, effervescent liquid lapped the glass, smearing the sides thickly. He was quite sure it was not a lotion one could purchase at Kirk's Imperial Hardware and General Store in town. "No thank you, Mr Haimona," he muttered. "I have some embrocation with me."

Haimona shrugged and slid the bottle back into the pouch. Then he retrieved a pipe from another hidden pocket, lit it, and began to smoke.

Suddenly it was dark. The purple haze of dusk had been fleeting and momentary: now the sky was frayed blackness, punctured by a thousand silver dots. The temperature fell rapidly. Shadows played on the tussock grass stretching out before them; strange, mythical shapes whirling on the charcoaled carpet, recently cleared by some unknown farmer. To Sanderson, glancing up briefly from Albert, it seemed as though

Haimona was a weird, other-world conductor, beating out a rhythm for the unknown, untamed shapes with his pipe. Haimona's eyes were closed.

Albert cried suddenly and reared up, flanks shuddering. Embrocation gleamed on his fetlock like goose fat on a Christmas bird. The animal panted and tossed his head for a second, white flecks flying, and was then still. A heavy silence slid down upon the travellers. For a moment, Sanderson felt completely cut off from the world. His eyes strained in the evening gloom, seeking out the station. It was about two miles away and he would have to walk.

They set off. Sanderson lit a small lantern and held it low by his side to mark out their steps. It cast a sallow ring on the ground, encircling both his and Haimona's feet. Haimona walked in lengthy strides, murmuring quietly to his horse every now and then. Sanderson glanced at him, baffled that the Māori would give up the comfort of his own ride to keep him company. Sanderson could think of no human connection between them except, maybe, given where they met, the need for a certain type of release. Since leaving Christchurch, Sanderson had longed to see the back of the man, though he hadn't quite been able to shake him off. He remembered how he had tried to slip away from the boarding house and the annoyance he felt when, turning in his saddle, he saw Haimona following at some distance.

"Why don't you ride?" he barked now. But he couldn't look at Haimona directly and stared instead down at the circle of light. "There's no need to walk alongside me."

Haimona gave an easy shrug and continued his slow lumber. The ground seemed to be swallowed by his gait, passing through his body and lit momentarily by the orange compass at his feet. "Better this way," he said, without explaining what he meant. His hand drifted out to stroke Albert again.

The station blinked up ahead. Sanderson wasn't sure if the sight was welcoming or a warning: there was no comfort in the knowledge he was near home. He thought of Sarah, probably in bed reading or, more likely, staring at the wallpaper as the wind pushed through the wooden slats. She slept a lot these days, crumpled on the iron frame. Sanderson's fingers would sink into her flesh late at night. She was a series of creases and rolls, and folded away places. But Sarah hadn't always been so. On their first night together, within the seclusion of their married quarter onboard the emigrant ship, she had removed her corset to reveal fragile ribs and a flat stomach beneath. After the corset, came the unbinding of the fabric wrapping her breasts, and she emerged from her hooped skirt, naked and trembling, blinking like a chick emerging from its egg.

The sensations aroused by her disrobing in their cramped, swaying cabin had taken William by surprise—he had not expected to feel that way about *her*. Sanderson thought he had taken Sarah off her parents' hands as an act of charity to them and convenience for himself. He did want sons, after all. But she served a greater purpose than he could have imagined—after their wedding he did not visit a boarding house for several months, not even after their emigrant ship had docked at Lyttleton.

His fist tightened around Albert's bridle. Their wedding day had not gone smoothly. Sarah had clung to her mother, and her mother to her. He had overheard them whispering after the service, when Sanderson had been thanking the minister and when Sarah should have been by his side. Instead she had stood apart, fingers plucking the new wedding band on her finger. Sarah's mother, thin and shabbily dressed, had babbled a warning about the married couple's first evening together, and Sanderson caught a glimpse of Sarah's horror-struck face. She had kept her lips pursed together that first night, silent but not resisting, rolling with the ship. In the morning she had not met his gaze. She wept for her mother for several weeks while the ship ploughed on relentlessly through the waves.

He was sure that one of Miss Swainson's girls had been on their boat. Of course, the single women had been separated from the married quarters, and carefully marshalled by two stout matrons, but still—a girl he had visited just last month seemed familiar. Naturally, she had not let on, even if she did recognise him. Instead she had smiled the whole evening, a gold tooth shining out in the darkness. She had not pursed her lips together, as Sarah had done. She had murmured encouragement and allowed him to caress the red lace of her nightgown. Something about her allowed him to leave all inhibitions at her doorway. He had paid the woman handsomely in the morning. A pity she had not been available last night.

Suddenly Haimona spoke. "I hadn't seen you at Miss Swainson's before." His disembodied voice rang out from the darkness conversationally but Sanderson almost stumbled. The Māori's words appalled him. How dare he remind him—an English gentleman!—about the circumstances of their meeting? But he had barely time to react before Haimona spoke again.

"Your English women. I see them getting off the boats, hoping to find husbands or work. Did so many expect to be earning their keep with their bodies?" And the Māori cleared his throat, the harsh sound carrying across the plains.

The temperature seemed to have dropped to below freezing. Sanderson drew up sharply. This really was outrageous. He brought the lamp up to his shoulder, swinging it around so its yellow light was cast against Haimona's face. Haimona's pipe was still in his mouth, pursed between blue lines that met at his lips. The Māori's eyes narrowed against the glare.

"A gentleman—a gentleman does not *speak* about such things!" Sanderson spluttered, heart pounding. "I'll thank you to keep your remarks to yourself, especially if I am to be forced to give you shelter!" Goosebumps pricked his arms as he wondered if Haimona would repeat his remarks at the station. Sarah was not a problem. But Sanderson did not think he could bear the smug glances of the shearers.

Haimona slowly drew the pipe from his mouth. His brown eyes studied the Englishman's face, taking in the grey bristles and thinning hair. "You have a wife at home, yes?" he asked quietly. "As do I. Yet we are drawn to these other women. I sell them lace that they drape over their bodies. They pay well. Sometimes I am offered more but I cannot accept. I have a wife in the north. But I still sell them lace, coming back to them month after month. Do you?"

Sanderson took a step back now, shocked beyond words. The Māori was clearly mad. He may have spent time bargaining with townsfolk and farmers, but he had learnt none of their English ways. The services of these women were not to be mentioned, ever—not even in those exclusive clubs back home from which Sanderson had been excluded. Nor should a man mention his wife in the same conversation. Decent women, after all, were ignorant about these matters. And Sanderson remembered the whispers between Sarah and her mother on their wedding day.

Haimona's face was impassive. He shrugged. "No matter. We will not speak of it again. I have some things to sell and then I will return home. I have been away for too long." He raised the pipe to his mouth, but paused. "Does your wife wear lace?"

Sanderson hit him. He hadn't expected to and it was at the full extent of his reach. But the blow struck home, glancing off Haimona's jaw and driving the Māori's head to the side. The pipe dropped to the earth with a soft thump and was lost to view. Sanderson, panting, moved in for a second attempt, fist pulled ready. There was a pounding in his ears and a remote part of his mind screeched for him to stop—these natives could be dangerous. But something had become detached inside and was no longer anchored to that repressed core. He felt delirious with violence. Albert harrumphed nervously.

Then Haimona turned to face him and the anger in Sanderson's breast and throat died. Blood seeped from a corner of Haimona's mouth, snaking down his chin. Images of red lace draped over the end of a bed bloomed in Sanderson's mind. His shoulders slumped heavily.

The Englishman and Māori stared at each other for a long time. Albert's tail switched, eyes flicking between the two. The orange light of the lantern drew a circle around them. Beyond the orb was only darkness, save for the twinkling station up ahead. They were quite cut off from all company. *This native could kill me if he wanted and no one would know*, Sanderson thought. But he did not feel fear; instead, only embarrassment that his life could end in such a way—he could just imagine the newspaper reports and the incredulous gasps of Harding's bankers. They stood for a long while, Māori and Englishman, caught in that moment.

MISS SWAINSON'S GIRL

Night fell quickly in Christchurch. She could be sitting at her dresser, pinning up her hair, listening to the ebb and flow of the boarding house on George Street as it came alive for the evening, when darkness would swallow her room. A year ago, on the first night she opened her room for business, the speed of nightfall had taken her by surprise. One moment she was winding red lace about her throat at the mirror, the next she had been plunged into blackness. She remembered how she had gasped and fumbled for a lamp. She had been panicked, sure that Oliver had found her, and that he had covered the lights. But the boarding house had droned on, voices lapping up the stairs as business was conducted as usual. Miss Swainson continued to welcome fresh callers at the door, channelling them into the warm body of the house. Oliver was—hopefully—far away, and soon the bedside lamp cast a reassuring glow across the flecked wallpaper.

She lit the oil in the lamp before darkness fell. The merry glass cylinder was almost the only bright thing in the room. It shone out like a beacon, casting red and blue glints of light across the mirror, picking out Phoebe's one gold tooth. She had insisted on having it, despite it being so startlingly obvious—it served as a reminder of Oliver's fists and why she left. And yet, she was not as tired, as rinsed out as the other girls, with their own scars and marks. Phoebe's skin was white and clear, mostly unblemished. Tonight, though, she had a bruise, a thumbprint on her cheek from a customer who paid extra to hold her face tightly. Like the gold tooth, the mark lingered stubbornly, warning her that one day someone might want to hold her by the throat.

Phoebe touched the lace at her neck. A recent guest, a man she was sure she recognised from the crossing, had worked up his courage by running the lace edges of her nightgown through his fingers before lying down next to her. Oliver had given her lace, too, once upon a time. He had pressed a handkerchief into her hand during the trip out on the *Empress* after slipping unseen down to the single women's quarters. The handkerchief was a token, he had said, to show the honour of his intentions. He was without money or the promise of a position in New Zealand, but she was to read the purity of his intentions in the whiteness of the cloth, he said. Hidden away in the claustrophobic box that served as Phoebe's cabin, he whispered these words like an incantation. These days, Phoebe bought red lace from the Māori who visited Miss Swainson's. Oliver's handkerchief had been lost, left behind in the scramble to escape him.

It was a new piece of lace that she wore tonight. Last night the boarding house had been visited by a group of shearers, desperate to spend money on something other than grog or their horses. A couple had been rough, made clumsy by the long absence of women. Some girls had trinkets stolen and clothes ripped. Phoebe herself had a nightgown torn and finally closed her door after four in the morning. Longing to collapse into bed, she had forced herself to change the sheets and wash with oil and vinegar. The concoction stained her underwear and stung, but she continued to use it, not least because it awoke an ache in her abdomen that nearly always reminded her of Belle. Dark haired and pink, Belle had arrived noisily fifteen months ago, smeared with blood and searching for Phoebe's breast. She had throbbed with life, churning the sheets of her crib with fat heels as she demanded milk, milk, milk. Sometimes, even now, the cry of a baby in the street below would bring heat to Phoebe's chest. Her body pulsed with memory. But her heart beat with relief that, so far, the oil and vinegar wash had kept further babies at bay.

She had put the last pin in her hair when someone knocked on her door. Miss Swainson stood in the archway, slightly out of breath from taking all three flights of stairs up to Phoebe's room. Her enormous, solid bust strained at her corset, pulling the fabric of her dress so tight that it appeared to be painted on. Her waist was thick and accentuated by a wide black band. She no longer worked. Five fatherless children, four of whom had died at birth, had weakened her body. Now, she was the figurehead of the boarding house, both leader and protector, steering her girls through the waves of clients, police visits and proselytising members of women's societies. A collection of keys and a small money pouch jangled at her hip, their tinny, clashing sounds speaking of entry to the boarding house's secret places. Somewhere amongst that bundle was a key for Phoebe's room and her rent would be in Miss Swainson's purse. Once a week, Miss Swainson's surviving son deposited the takings at Hardings Bank on Main Street, dressed for the occasion in an expensive coat and leather shoes. He had been educated privately, Phoebe had heard, but was not above demanding free service from the girls from time to time. He was territorial and resisted the police's demands to inspect them, raising his voice in the doorway so neighbours could hear his threats to name those who frequented the house.

Miss Swainson spoke slowly, trying to control her breath.

"Delivery for you," and she held out a thin wooden box. It was about as long as her hand. "There was no name—a man brought it to the door."

Phoebe took the box, turning it over. It had been roughly made from uneven bits of wood and was slightly wider at one end. *It looks like a tiny coffin*, she thought, puzzled. There were no markings and something clattered inside.

"There was no message with it, Miss Swainson?"

The stout lady shook her head. "And I didn't see the man who delivered it. Marianne received him, said he sounded like a new chum from Liverpool. He asked for you by name."

The breath left Phoebe's throat in a sudden rush. Oliver was from Liverpool.

The warmth of the attic room pressed up against her, squeezing the air from her lungs in a frightening, yet familiar way. As a child, she had once been tempted to step onto the ice of the local pond—it had cracked and given way, and she had slipped into the glacial waters below. Her brother had been quick to haul her out, no harm done, but the memory of that sharp, crushing cold lingered. Moments of shock returned her to those childhood waters, to that feeling of suffocation. She had felt it when she realised a baby was coming and when she discovered that Oliver's promises of love were slippery, as unstable as the ice on the pond. Stepping off the *Empress* and onto Auckland harbour, Oliver had pushed her towards a hotel, where he emptied the meagre contents of her purse onto the bar. Phoebe had watched, aware that, this time, her brother was not there to haul her back.

"Thank you, Miss Swainson," she said quietly. "I will be ready to receive visitors in a few moments."

Miss Swainson nodded curtly and left, wheezing down the stairs. Phoebe closed her door slowly and sat down on the bed.

She stared at the box. The rough wood was not unlike that of her trunk, now covered with a silk cloth beside the dresser. The travelling box had been a leaving gift from her father, hammered and beaten into shape with his cobbler's hands. He had carved her initials on the top, the smoothness of the grooves offering his tacit, hopeful approval of his daughter's venture into a new world. But now she lied to him in letters home, giving no hint of Belle, his only grandchild.

Oliver had something to do with the small box she now held, Phoebe was certain. He came from Liverpool, like her, and must have been the caller at the door. She glanced around nervously, seeing his shape in the shadows. He must have tracked her from Auckland. She shuddered, wondering if any of the other girls had been with him, but she would have surely heard about it. The violence carried in his narrow frame had a way of oozing from his pores: meanness slid from his body in sly pinches and fists in soft flesh. He did not know about Belle. She had left before her stomach grew big, hiding herself in the depths of an old coat, slipping out one night while Oliver was in the hotel, drinking and fighting.

The last time she had stared so intently at a box, it was one she had filled with Belle's belongings. Knitted hats and shawls had been laid carefully alongside a photograph of them both, taken on Auckland's quayside. She had also bought a newspaper, to mark the date of their separation, and placed this in the box. Finally she included Belle's rattle, a simple metal toy bought in a shop on Queen's Street. She had the box nailed shut and took a dray to Onehunga, to a house tucked away down a side street. A thin, worn woman, so much at odds with the revered reputation whispered amongst the unmarried and desperate, answered the door. A child made a happy noise in the background and a warming smell of cabbage drifted from the kitchen. The woman didn't seem surprised to see Phoebe, and into her hands Phoebe deposited the box, a promise of monthly cheques and, with a rendering that tore her heart, Belle. The following morning she left for Christchurch. She sometimes wondered if Belle remembered her.

And what if Oliver had found her child, *their* child? Perched like a bird on the edge of her bed, Phoebe moved nervously. He hadn't come looking for *her* when she left in the middle of the night, and he could have found her if he had really wanted. Alone and without friends in Auckland, Phoebe spent those first few nights away in a brown, stale hotel room, paid for out of savings scraped together from coins left in Oliver's beer-splattered trousers. If he had searched the hotels by the harbour he could easily have found her. But she had been more careful when it came to her lying in. A job in a milliner's shop on Shortland Street had allowed her to save enough for bed in a discreet refuge out of the city. Her time there had been daunting. A woman in the next room had been confined the night before Belle arrived and delivered of a dead child. Holding her own baby in her arms, the neighbour's screams rattling the walls, Phoebe could not then imagine being separated from her child. Not then. But within weeks the threat of destitution and the scorn of the well-to-do towards fallen women, like herself, had thrust Belle into the house at Onehunga and propelled Phoebe to the boarding house in Christchurch.

If Oliver had found Belle ... if he had harmed her after all Phoebe had done—was *still* doing—to keep her safe … the heat of the attic room closed in and Phoebe remembered the glacial pond from her youth again. In her mind's eye she saw Belle as she remembered her—just weeks old and dressed in white—and the two memories converged. Belle became white foam on icy waters, her skirt fanning out in the water as she floated, drifted, away from her mother.

An old anvil, gifted by Phoebe's father and used to shape tough shoe leather, stood by the bed. For those men who noticed, it was an item of curiosity, but for Phoebe it served as protection—or, at least, it provided the façade that she could fight off a client. As Belle glided away from her on her frigid path, she grabbed the anvil. The wooden box was thrown down onto the floor and Phoebe raised the heavy iron over her head.

From the splinters, something shiny glinted in the dimness. It was a rattle. It caught the light from her lamp, bouncing silver shapes on the flecked wallpaper.

DOTTIE

Because she needed to convince herself she was doing the Lord's work, the bedroom door was kept tightly shut and Evie was encouraged to play noisily. The woman learnt to cut off the needle-like fingers of worry that plucked at her insides and, on days when Evie was here and the babies were quiet, she was almost certain she was doing what God wanted. How could she not be, when so many of Auckland's destitute came to her door, answering the discreet notice carried in the *Observer*?

"Lonely widow of independent means seeks child to care for or adopt. All cases considered. Reply care of Mrs Amelia Gray, Cameron Street, Onehunga."

God must be helping her, she reasoned on some days, for the women came. They carried, in one hand, carpet bags of belongings—clothes, rattles, photographs in valuable frames—and, in the other, they held their children. Some were just days old; the eldest had been a boy of fourteen months, though he had been hard work and difficult to subdue. A few women handed money and babe over immediately, reluctant to linger. Others came back for many a "last kiss". And Mrs Gray let them. And, beneath it all, it was understood that the child would quickly disappear into that room upstairs, and go to the Lord. Their belongings would be dispatched to one of Auckland's many pawnbrokers or buried in the garden.

But it was harder to convince herself of the Lord's grace at night. At night it stayed hot and she could not sleep. The sun had warned her early of its power. Soon after landing on the quayside it had stopped her husband's heart, his life evaporating through his skin until he became a dried-up parcel of a man, ready to tumble into an early grave.

A cake stood on the kitchen table. Mrs Gray saw it as she entered the room, straightening her skirts. She was particularly smart this morning. Mrs Ellis of the Women's Christian Temperance Society was due to visit, to solicit support for the Good Templars, no doubt. Mrs Gray had the air of money, though no one in Auckland's young society was sure where it came from. The cake was for Evie who was eight today. The girl was polite: a pleasure to care for while her mother worked. It lifted her heart to hear the child play about the house and her presence comforted some of the desperate that came to the door. At times Mrs Gray clung to Evie, in a way that bewildered the girl; she just wanted to be close to that warmth, that life pulsing through a checked dress. But on other days, she shrunk from Evie, frightened by her unfettered zest for experience.

The baker had delivered the cake yesterday and it now sat on the table, a waiting promise. It was smothered in white icing, domes whipped upright into plump curves. The sugary mix wasn't soft when Mrs Gray touched it. A piece broke off in her fingers, brittle and bone-like. She laid it down with distaste and glanced out the window at the garden.

The patch of earth behind the house was stark in its difference from the well-maintained flower beds at the front door. There, begonias and roses from home thrust their faces out proudly towards the street. Look at us, they seemed to shout—it takes effort to tend to us, to help us grow, but here we are, nonetheless. And yet, out the back, the garden was unkempt and wild. Rubble and vines competed for space in a narrow strip, tumbling together in a tight embrace. Tussock grass rose so high in places that it would come up to Evie's chest, if she was allowed to play there. Her aunt warned her off, though, restricting her to the house. Looking through the kitchen window, Mrs Gray picked out a couple of small mounds of earth. They were still well hidden in the undergrowth.

Mrs Gray moved to the sideboard, taking out her best china and embroidered napkins. She would offer Mrs Ellis a piece of cake which, no doubt, the older woman would accept eagerly. Those on a mission could always be tempted with good things to eat. Once a policeman had come to her door, suspicious but apologetic. He had questions about the steady stream of women who visited the house on Cameron Street. Fortunately the babies had been dosed that morning and the door to their room was tightly shut. He spoke briefly of searching the house, but she distracted him with English chocolates and sugary tea. He was a poor man, after all.

Mrs Gray laid the china plates out on the kitchen table and took out two silver spoons from a drawer. A bottle of Garner's Cordial rolled to the front. It was almost empty. There were only three children upstairs at the moment, but one, an unusually hearty girl of six months, had persistently vomited the mixture back. Mrs Gray was sure the child did it deliberately, resisting the liquid sleep. The girl's mother had arrived at her door late one evening. She'd murmured the child's name softly, repeatedly, before handing her over. Mrs Gray had tried to avoid hearing her—names meant identity and identity meant attachment—but Dottie was heavy and determinedly *present*. Usually the children came when their mothers were at the end of their endurance, the push of infant bones under their skin telling a multitude of sad stories. But not Dottie: this child was plump and babbling. She had grabbed at Mrs Gray's arms as she held her, and Mrs Gray felt the strength in her little bones. And, although Dottie had waned a little in the three days she'd been upstairs, the child hung on. Mrs Gray had to force her to swallow the cordial, pinning Dottie's arms by her side for longer than she liked. She didn't like to touch the children.

It was almost nine o'clock and Mrs Ellis would be here soon. She had been once before, last summer, and they had taken tea in the parlour. A restless woman, Mrs Ellis unnerved Mrs Gray with her vitality. She was always moving—hands, eyes, all caught up in a fluttering cycle of motion. She had admired Mrs Gray's cushions, and then her books, and then her collection of icons on the walls, moving rapidly between them until Mrs Gray felt quite dizzy. Mrs Gray disliked sudden, hurried movements or bursts of speech: they did something unsettling to her stomach. She hoped the cake would be a distraction and keep Mrs Ellis pinned to the kitchen table for the duration of her visit.

A muffled cry from upstairs: Dottie again. Glancing at the small clock beside the stove, Mrs Gray saw she had only a few minutes before Mrs Ellis was due to arrive. She snatched the cordial bottle from the drawer and hurried from the room. At the foot of the stairs Dottie's cries sounded louder—unlike the other babies, she had not become quieter as time wore on. Weaker children whimpered towards the end, a cat-like noise Mrs Gray could ignore. But Dottie seemed to have been incensed by the denial of milk and, when awake, wailed constantly and piercingly, an arching sound that raised goosebumps on Mrs Gray's arms.

The sound reminded Mrs Gray of the first child she sent to the Lord. Her sister's eldest, conceived and born in sin. A boy, puny and belligerent, determined to scratch his way to life despite his mother's disinterest and rejection. He became an opportunity for Mrs Gray, widowed and penniless. She offered to help and her sister's lover, a wealthy married man, had gladly handed over enough money to smooth away the problem. Sometimes she wondered if he would have looked like Evie, had he been allowed to live.

With her hand on the door handle, the crying stopped. Dottie did this, a cat-and-mouse game that made Mrs Gray feel as though the baby was in charge. Not *her*, the woman holding the glass bottle. Wanting to preserve the supply of Garner's, Mrs Gray had spent the first day Dottie was present in the house darting up and down the stairs, exasperated but bemused by this child. If she went into the room, Dottie would smile up at her from her crib made from a wooden box and lined with straw. Toothy, round-faced and grinning through the incredulity of her situation, Dottie wormed her way through the fibrous surface of Mrs Gray's heart. But still the woman pinned her down and dosed the baby with Garner's.

The child whimpered as Mrs Gray opened the door. The room was dark, heavy curtains blocking out all light. The air was stale and thick with decay. Babies had succumbed here, some very quickly, their tiny bodies leaving faint odours. Dottie lay in the middle of the room almost hidden by shadows. To her left and right were the prostrate forms of younger children. From their rigid shapes, Mrs Gray could tell they had passed to the Lord in the night. It had happened quickly but unsurprisingly, for both had arrived sick and emaciated. Not fat and hearty like Dottie.

But when she looked closely at the child, something had changed. Dottie's eyes had glassed over and her lips were dry and taut.

Mrs Gray picked her up. The baby was much lighter than when she had arrived three days before. She wouldn't need to swallow much of the cordial for it to be over. Mrs

Gray almost felt relieved and raised the bottle to Dottie's lips. But as the baby's lips parted, hoping for milk, she thought of Evie. Fervent, earnest Evie, roaring with life and joy. She imagined the girl's face when she saw her birthday cake, and how she would sit excitedly down at the table, her own cupid-bow mouth open to eat.

Something creased inside: a cord of self-control, stretched by the pressure of the last eight years. It buckled and her insides felt as though they had turned into molten mass. A sour taste filled her mouth. Without realising what she was doing, she dropped the bottle of Garner's and pressed Dottie to her breast. She smelled unpleasant—she had not been cleaned during that time—but Mrs Gray squeezed her tightly. Dottie looked up, eyes rolling slightly in the back of her head.

Mrs Gray stumbled from the room, flinging the door open wide. Sunlight streamed in, picking out tiny particles of dust and illuminating the darkened shapes of Dottie's two companions. They lay in silent repose as Dottie was carried down the stairs by Mrs Gray, now sobbing freely. She burst into the kitchen, sweeping aside the items on the kitchen table—cake, plates, spoons crashed to the floor. She lay Dottie carefully down on the wooden surface and stripped her. She then filled the sink with water and, plunging embroidered napkins into the water, began to wash the child.

Dottie watched. The rush of movement had snapped her attention back onto the world and her eyes cleared a little. Seeing this, Mrs Gray smiled and cooed. "Baby, baby."

She dried the infant on a kitchen towel. A bottle of milk stood in the corner of the room, the coolest place in the house and, sitting on the floor with Dottie on her knee, she retrieved a spoon and began to tip some of the liquid into the child's mouth. Dottie swallowed hungrily. Mrs Gray's tears dripped down onto the child's head.

And then there was a movement in the doorway. Mrs Gray's head snapped up. A woman stood there—Mrs Ellis—her face pale and shocked. In her hand she held a bible and velvet purse. The two women stared at each over the debris on the kitchen floor.

Mrs Ellis stood rigid, stiller than Mrs Gray had ever seen her. *Like a pillar of salt*, she thought a little hysterically, the chiding weight of the baby lying heavily in her arms. She looked down. The milk had brought colour to Dottie's cheeks and her eyes were round and bright. She glared up at the broken woman holding her so tightly, and Mrs Gray wondered at the barefacedness of the child. She carried no hint of sin in her flesh, and yet— Dottie's skin, satin to the touch, reminded Mrs Gray of a priest's cloak. She quailed, feeling undone, *judged*, by this soft, warm bundle, and thought of the babies that had gone before.

"Where did this child come from?"

Mrs Ellis had regained some composure. She stepped further into the kitchen, straddling broken china with her unfashionable skirts. Her glance switched rapidly from Mrs Gray to Dottie. Mrs Gray looked at Mrs Ellis dazedly.

"From upstairs," she whispered. She watched as Mrs

Ellis sped from the room. For a woman who was never still, Mrs Ellis's step was purposeful—until she entered the silent bedroom, whereupon she stumbled and fell back down to the kitchen in an uneven rush.

"Mrs Gray! There are—"

"You do not need to say it," Mrs Gray said. She drew herself up, getting shakily to her feet. She felt as though she had become transparent and shapeless. She sat down awkwardly on a kitchen chair. Dottie, sated for now, had fallen asleep. Mrs Gray laid her gently down upon the table. "Would you like to sit, Mrs Ellis? I cannot offer you tea, I'm afraid."

Mrs Ellis's breath was coming in short gasps, her chest rising and falling like the bellows of a church organ. She sat down uncertainly, her eyes travelling over the sleeping baby. She clutched her bible.

The tighter Mrs Ellis coiled around that holy book, the looser Mrs Gray felt. Her very bones felt fluid and malleable. It was as though she was changing shape inside her skin. She could see into the parlour over Mrs Ellis's shoulder. Silver frames and trinkets rested alongside crucifixes on the mantelpiece.

Mrs Gray began to speak. "You came for a donation, yes? I don't suppose you want one now." She reached out to stroke Dottie. "Mrs Ellis, please understand. This colony grinds the very life from you. The heat. The pressure of society luncheons and calling cards. Growing the brightest flowers. Observing the unspoken rules relating to behaviour and faith." A sigh. "Some came out here thinking they'd left those shackles on the quayside, but convention *floats*. It emigrates right alongside us, ready to trumpet any misdemeanour or indiscretion. Like my sister's."

Mrs Ellis wrung her hands, and her skin shone. "Mrs Gray, do you run a baby farm? Please, tell me you don't," and she squeezed her hands together in prayer.

"I've read that's what they call it," Mrs Gray said slowly. "Yes, I suppose I do. I hadn't really intended to but—I wanted to help my sister." She found herself crying again. "I told her to come out to New Zealand. Before Henry died, I was so full of hope. I thought this place was wonderful. It didn't seem to matter where you came from, as long as you were willing to work. You could make your own kingdom of heaven out in the backblocks or right here in the city. But Amy became—what do you call it? A fallen woman. She found—we found—that everyone judges out here, just the same. *I* judged her."

"This is a wicked thing," Mrs Ellis mumbled, rocking slowly. "Behold, children are a heritage from the Lord, the fruit of the womb, a reward."

"Yes, I see that now," Mrs Gray said and drew Dottie to her again. "I should have done so all along. But what were we to do? My sister didn't feel as though her child was a reward. If Amy had kept the boy—if I'd allowed him to live—she would have been a sinner. And she would never have found work or a husband." Dottie's eyes fluttered behind blue-veined lids and Mrs Gray felt the matching beat of her own heart. "And then there would be no Evie. So the boy—he had to die, don't you see? To have a child out of wedlock is a sin."

Mrs Ellis shook her head vehemently but her voice stayed low. "I came out here full of hope, like you. I have been disappointed—by the intemperance and grog shops. And I understand the resentment of women enslaved by their bodies and the will of men but—there are other ways. Not this."

"Maybe God would have forgiven my sister," Mrs Gray said, her tone matching that of Mrs Ellis. "Maybe our society would have looked kindly on Amy, and her boy, and she could have made a life here. But she wouldn't have married and had my niece, treasure that she is."

"Her boy might have been equally so," Mrs Ellis whispered. "Only, you never gave him that chance, did you? And the others. What have you to say of the others that have died in that room upstairs?"

Of those Mrs Gray could say nothing. Her sister had not been discreet and word had spread; a week had not passed after the death of Amy's son before another woman appeared on her doorstep, child in one hand and coins in the other. It was too tempting to a woman newly widowed and frightened. And now, with Dottie nestled on her lap, the child's warmth spreading like a stain through her thighs, the Lord finally spoke to Mrs Gray. It was the first time she had heard him and He spoke in a much clearer way than she ever expected. Mrs Gray listened, as He told her that, now, behind her, gathered a cloud. A collection of souls, of the children she had despatched. They had come to fetch her. They would wait patiently, for Mrs Ellis to leave or have her arrested, and for Dottie to be saved. And then Mrs Gray was to go to them and to Him. It would be easy and only what she deserved. Mrs Gray licked her dry lips, and thought of the bottle of Garner's Cordial lying in the room upstairs. She felt something akin to relief.

PORT AND ORANGES

In the early hours of the morning, as the boarding house settled into sleep and the visitors had been sated, Miss Abigail Swainson liked to retire to her sitting room, lower her ample frame into a deep easy chair, unlace her corset and boots, and sip a large glass of port. She had just one crystal glass left; the others had been hawked, pawned, or smashed along the winding path her life had taken in this odd colony. For Miss Swainson, the loss of such comforts had begun early; the roll and surge of the three-month crossing from Gravesend had swallowed books and trinkets, and had ruined silk dresses with big gobs of salty spit. Necessity and expedience quickly became the dominant impulses of the new chum docking at Auckland harbour. So now, at Miss Swainson's table, chipped china plates sat alongside cheap wooden platters, and faithful old jam jars were as usefully employed as cut-glass flutes. Still. Odd moments demanded a degree of luxury. Miss Swainson enjoyed nothing more after an evening of greeting clients and soothing the fractious spirits of her girls than to raise the Edinburgh crystal to her lips.

The sitting room was private, of course, and strictly out of bounds to all, except Charles. Not that he encroached upon his mother's space too much, apart from when his own supplies of grog were running low. Then, he would stay for a while, drinking port from a jam jar, idly stroking the rimu and pine chest of drawers of which Miss Swainson was so proud. She pretended not to notice when—usually about three in the morning and when he thought she had drifted off to sleep—Charles would disappear along the landing and knock on the door of whichever girl had dismissed her client and become free.

Tonight, Miss Swainson was especially tired. A recent hoard of shearers from Lake Coleridge had flooded the house just the night before, and their rowdiness demanded a firm hand. Stout with age and the thickness of experience, Miss Swainson had controlled the visitors with a variety of tactics: some were little more than boys and responded to a firm, maternal tone. They seemed unable to control their strong, angular bodies, and their eyes had a look of shock at the sheer elasticity of their limbs. Others were more advanced in years and arrogant with desire. A mixture of manipulation and coquetry was required in these cases, and a hushed word to her more experienced girls to hurry matters along.

This morning, tired though she was, listening to the occasional creak or groan as a client tumbled satisfactorily towards sleep, Miss Swainson was on her third glass of port and sleep was an elusive friend. A letter sat on the rimu chest. Forwarded on by the Lyttleton office, the letter had arrived two weeks ago, after a lengthy passage on the *Hawarden Castle* from Southampton. Dust from the alley had started to gather on the open pages.

A chill crept in from an open window; Miss Swainson rose from her chair and closed it, wrinkling her nose against the stench of manure and refuse from the street. An old cadger, slumped against a doorway somewhere, sang out drunkenly. Miss Swainson couldn't see him. A short distance from the main drag, the boarding house sat in blackness. Christchurch's respectable folk, keen to assert a connection with the pilgrims on one of the pioneering first ships could, if they wanted, pretend that places like Miss Swainson's house did not exist; and, mostly, that suited Miss Swainson just fine. She did yearn on occasion, though, to march her girls up Cashel Street, in their silks and feathers, shouting out the names of their pompous, shamefaced clients. The thought made her smile, looking out from her window. But, so late at night, Miss Swainson couldn't make out the dirt of the road. She experienced an unnerving sensation of vertigo slide over her, as though she was about to fall face first into nothing. She touched the glass, seeking reassurance in the cold transparency, and then backed into her room. Her chest hurt.

The chair was less welcoming as Miss Swainson eased herself onto the cushions. Her lungs were bothersome these days. Coughing, she leaned over awkwardly to light another lamp noting, not for the first time, that hers was not as bright as a lamp owned by one of her girls; whenever she entered the girl's room, Miss Swainson admired the pretty glass, with its clever knack of casting shards of blue, red and green around the room. Not that she ever said she liked it, of course. Detachment was crucial.

There was a knock at the door. Miss Swainson glanced at the bottle of port on the wooden trunk, which doubled up as a table. "Come in, Charles."

The door opened slowly—it was not Charles. Instead, one of her girls stood silently in the shadows, dressed in a white robe.

Miss Swainson got up as quickly as her frame allowed. "Eliza? What is it? One of the men?"

Eliza made a small, high-pitched noise, and Miss Swainson was reminded of the rats in the cellar, trapped by their gluttony in steel cages. She picked up her lamp and moved over to the doorway. Eliza's face was ashen and there were deep circles beneath her eyes. The girl trembled in the cool air and, when she rubbed her bare arms, her hands shook.

"It's not that, Ma'am," and she glanced down.

Sudden understanding—so sudden, Miss Swainson was almost sure she squinted. "No, it's something else, isn't it?"

With her compact hands, Miss Swainson eased the girl back into the corridor and closed the door to her sitting room. The women stood together on the icy landing, Miss Swainson holding the lamp up so that the walls became lacquered in orange shadows. "So. How long?"

Eliza had some awkward, flowery clips in her hair, pinning it back from her face rather savagely. Her features were taut, accentuating an already long nose and slightly protruding eyes. "Two months."

"Good," Miss Swainson said briskly. "There's still time. Hold this please." She passed the lamp over and returned to the sitting room. She opened one of the rimu drawers, searching for something. The pages of the letter were shuffled about by the motion. Miss Swainson paused, and then gathered the letter together again.

She returned to Eliza and handed over a blue glass bottle, half full. Eliza screwed up her eyes to read the label, drawing the lamp close. Looking at the girl's face, Miss Swainson was, for a mad moment, reminded of a clementine, squashed to a pulp and part of the refuse on the street below.

"Dr Liberi's Restorative Water?" Eliza read slowly.

"Removes blockages, restores regularity, all done discreetly and without recourse to a physician," Miss Swainson intoned. "Three of my girls have used it just this year."

Eliza twisted in her nightgown, buckling awkwardly like a vine around a timber fence. "Thank you," she whispered. "It's good of you, but … it's not that."

"Oh. Something else, then?"

"No. I mean … well, I don't know what I mean." Eliza handed the blue bottle over. Whatever she was trying to say, her meaning on *that* particular point was clear.

Miss Swainson rubbed the tonic thoughtfully. "Let's see. Has he said he'll stand by you?"

Eliza inhaled quickly, the delicate bones at her throat blanching her skin. The lamp was at her side now, illuminating the walls to the left and right. The women stood in a thin shaft of light, a bright line between opposing spheres of darkness. "I haven't told him. But, I hoped ..."

Miss Swainson folded her arms across her large chest. The vulnerability of the girl blazed out and Miss Swainson thought for a moment that she would like to scoop her up and place her inside a glass bottle, like a firefly, safe from harm and admired from afar. "Eliza," she began slowly. "Do you think no other girl here has been in your position?"

Eliza hung her head.

"What if he's married?" Miss Swainson was aware that she sounded relentless. "Or just doesn't want to deal with the burden? You only have to look at the papers to see all those poor women, chasing after bounders who have deserted them."

"Phoebe manages it," Eliza said, looking up. "She does it on her own. She doesn't know I know, but she posts a letter every month to a woman in Auckland."

Ah, the girl with the beautiful lamp. These girls, they do have their secrets, and Miss Swainson shook her head. "Well, these things are never all they seem. But wouldn't you rather be without that worry? And, of course, you couldn't continue to work here once ... well, you won't stay a slip forever."

Eliza blinked. She had always disliked Miss Swainson's brash way of speaking and the way it cut through all artifice or fakery. Her speech, for example, made to all the new girls upon their arrival at the boarding house, was brutal and raw. "This is no game," she told them, often in the small parlour they all called "Customs and Exchange." There, they would meet the men before leading them to private quarters. Miss Swainson liked to sit the girls on the same horsehair seat that served the visitors. "You must leave all romantic notions at the door," she advised them, speaking firmly but not unkindly. "And forget the silly little rules of etiquette and decorum that dominated you before you came out. Do not try to be aloof or alluring—a true colonial has no time for that, and an Englishman will be reminded of the women he comes here to escape. Remember, you will be paid to perform a service, as distasteful as that may sound to some of you. And you will be paid well. Embrace it—money will set you free, and you might not have to stick at this for too long. Of course, you will pass on a portion of your takings to me. In exchange, I will keep you safe and will turn away anyone who is drunk, violent, or too hectoring. The church and temperance folk call here, but not often. I can't promise to keep away the inspectors, but if you stay off the streets, there will be less cause for you to be exposed to their questioning." Eliza had no idea to what Miss Swainson referred at this point, but the more seasoned of boarders later revealed the forced searches and bodily examinations.

But, despite Miss Swainson's words, on most days, Eliza was able to play a convincing little trick. She fooled herself that the visitors to her room were princes, and she was a trapped Rapunzel-like figure, waiting for the perfect knight to release her. The rotund shopkeepers and grubby coffee vendors became the princes that populated the nighttime stories of childhood. She tried to remember her mother's voice: "The lonely Prince of

Persia sought the company of his beautiful maiden, and was delighted to find himself in her arms again." The memory of her clever, sweet, buried mother gave her strength.

In recent days, though, that strength had seeped from her, and she wondered if she might collapse inwards, like a flower closing its petals for the last time. "I'm caught, aren't I, Miss Swainson?"

Miss Swainson rolled her lips into a tight line. "Think things through clearly, Eliza. That's all I can counsel you."

Eliza handed back the lamp. Her fingers were terribly cold. She offered up a small, strangely knowing smile to Miss Swainson, and slipped away into the blackness. An entreaty was on Miss Swainson's tongue for the briefest moment, a call for her to come back, out of the darkness—but the words were swallowed quickly, and Miss Swainson retreated to her room.

Jane, Helen, Caroline, and now Eliza. Miss Swainson sat back down in the easy chair and, despite her efforts, couldn't help but imagine the slow slide of Dr Liberi's magical potion cutting through her girls. The tonic was so euphemistically described in the *Press*—a "restorative water". Restorative of what, exactly? Of a bodily pattern, a rhythm, a moment of order before a new life began? Miss Swainson had poured out the doses for her girls; it smelled inoffensive, like water flavoured with lemons. She imagined it seeping outwards, prising the tender shoots of life from within and flushing them out.

Poor, sweetly beguiled Eliza, if she really did hope a man would rescue her from all this. Miss Swainson drank her port. The reality of children and men, she had found, were very different from the promise. A long time ago, with what was left of her savings, Miss Swainson had bought the boarding house, gliding along on a false wing of hope that it would be a family home. The married lover had made all kinds of promises, if only she would keep out of sight until matters could be settled with a barren but stout and immovable wife. Stupefied by the strangeness of this new land and what she thought was love, Miss Swainson had remained in the shadows, even when the size of her stomach made it difficult to sort the washing or bake bread.

The loss of her first child, three hours after birth, had been a terrible shock. And yet—it drew fresh affection from her lover, and led them to a different place, to a deeper understanding. They discovered each other anew in a new land. They took to walking, climbing the Port Hills and looking down on the sodden, mired streets of young Christchurch. Flat like a tablecloth, the land upon which the pioneers had settled stretched out towards the Southern Alps, and seemed ripe with possibility. Remembering, Miss Swainson shook her head at the foolishness. She was sure the wife would be discarded, scandal or no, and they would marry. The lover promised as much after the second son was born dead, then the third and the fourth. Finally, after Charles stubbornly refused to go the way of his brothers, the lover sold up and took his wife back to England.

England. When she thought of it, Miss Swainson no longer missed the smell of smoke and the knock-kneed shuffle up narrow, cobble-stone streets. After so many years away, Miss Swainson had to suppress a snigger when a caller eulogised romantically about the sweetness of English ferns and the song of a nightingale. Honestly, please, she felt like chortling, but tried to remember that this colony attracted all types of emigrant. The England she had left behind was rather different to the flowery ideal recalled by her visitors. Her England was a buttoned-up drawing room, where the labour with which tapestries and china were bought was not mentioned, ever. Father had once taken her on a tour of his factory, where she watched sullen-faced women chase after wooden sticks wrapped in cotton. They looked at her with hatred—a look she threw right back. The nearest she got to cotton now was on the pillowcases and bed sheets.

And so, in the circular way that thoughts go, Miss Swainson found herself returning to the letter resting on the rimu dresser. Such a beautiful item of furniture, bought when she was pregnant for the first time, to store tiny clothes. Raw, colonial hope followed the grain of wood, but the sheen had been rubbed away. Now, the missive from England sat on top. An answer was required, a decision must be made. That much, at least, was clear from her sister-in-law's terse prose. Miss Swainson could not help but smile. How she must have hated writing it! The barrenness of these women was like a poison to them; their bodies could not, would not sustain life, so they nurtured bile instead. Her lover's wife, her brother's wife—they simmered with resentment towards the flighty, the immoral, the fertile. So. Would she consider coming back, taking up her dear departed brother's reins and overseeing the mill?

Pondering, Miss Swainson looked up as Charles entered the room. He did so without knocking, and sat down opposite his mother. His hair was unkempt, his cravat loose. "Have you any port?"

Miss Swainson motioned over to the bottle and watched as her son poured out a large amount into a jam jar. He drank and sat back in his chair, his thick, round head resting on the fabric.

"I've had a letter," Miss Swainson said slowly. "From your Aunt Susanne."

"Oh?" Charles's eyes were shut.

"Uncle Frederick has died."

Charles snapped his head forward. His eyes were now open and wide. Miss Swainson could see he knew what that meant. "How—sad," he said, his voice looping oddly.

"Yes. Isn't it?" Miss Swainson traced a finger around the top of her glass. "Well, of course, it does raise a number of interesting questions."

Charles raised his round chin in mock surprise. How do you mean, he gestured.

Miss Swainson wondered if she should play a little game with her dearest, only son. His eagerness for money rolled off him in sweaty waves. "Your aunt has asked if I could go home. Take up the reins at the mill. Oh, I don't know Charles. I've become so fond of my life here."

"Yes, yes. But—"

"I mean, my girls. What would they do? They come to me with all their troubles."

"You are a great listener, Mother. But with that kind of finance back home—"

"For example, Eliza was here only a few moments ago."

"Eliza?" Charles leaned forward in his chair.

"The young girl on the landing below. Long curly hair. She's got herself into trouble, hasn't she?" Miss Swainson sighed dramatically. "I offered to help, but she seems to have some false hope about the fellow concerned."

Charles's eyes bulged like saucers, put out for the cats and fat with milk. Tiny pearls appeared on his top lip.

"She isn't too far gone, there's still something that can be done—" and Miss Swainson stopped, noticing her son's stricken face. For the second time that night, a light popped inside her skull. She fell back in her chair, her chest tight. "Ah. Charles. I see."

Charles shook his head rapidly. "I can't—no, it wouldn't be possible—she never said—"

Miss Swainson breathed deeply. She looked over at the letter on the drawers and thought of her long-ago lover. Then she looked back to her son, dishevelled and undone in his expensive clothes. "Yes," she said quietly. "This does rather change things, doesn't it?"

TENDERNESS

Later, when Mrs Ellis allowed herself to recall that day, it struck her how odd and strangely wonderful it had been to discover such small moments of tenderness. They sprang up, unexpected and fountain-like. Of course, outwardly, Mrs Ellis did not reveal their effect and maintained a stoic self-control as the day progressed. After giving her details, she stood quietly to the side as the constable completed his work and escorted the suspect, Mrs Gray, from the premises. She was discreet as onlookers, neighbours, and those desperate to be shocked were shooed away. Then, unnoticed, she flagged down a dray on Manukau Road and took herself out of Onehunga, towards the throb of the city. She had no clear idea of where she was headed, and just muttered to the driver to head north. Shock had rubbed away the sharpness of her senses and sapped the energy from her legs; she felt as though she was in the sea, in the deep blue of the harbour, with water in her nose and mouth. Or that she was in a drugged sleep. But such a thought reminded her of the babies in Mrs Gray's house, so she pushed it away.

At the corner of Symonds Street and Karangahape Road she disembarked, emptying her purse into the driver's hands. The Domain was not far away, and Mrs Ellis had wandered there before. Today, however, she did not want to walk the greens, where cherry trees scented the air and the calm of the duck ponds was broken only by a feathery squabble. Mrs Ellis needed to be somewhere different, where she could sting herself back to clarity. The morning had been a blur. She headed towards the Symonds Street cemetery instead.

She passed the timber houses with their white balustrades and decking, along the wide brown street stained with horse manure. The edges of the hillside cemetery came right up to the pavement, the dead lapping at the frontiers of the living. Mrs Ellis swung open the wooden gate into the graveyard and stepped in. Moss and grass had already started to claim some headstones, and she had to lift her skirts and carefully pick her way through the gully. Built into terraces on sloping banks, tall and solid monuments stood to mark the slumber of Auckland's wealthy and respected. Other, smaller graves spoke of more muted grief but, Mrs Ellis was sure, of a sorrow felt just as keenly.

She paused in front of one simple grey slab, shaped like an open book. "Sacred to the memory of Angela Elizabeth Foster, departed 21 August 1871, aged five months. A precious dream." She said the words quietly. An open hearth, white rags drying in the heat, a bowl of watery porridge; the doctor coming but being able to do nothing—and then a tiny coffin lowered into the ground. Grey, long-ago days, when her mother had wrung her hands over an empty cradle and other, more recent moments that Mrs Ellis felt keenly had educated her that this was the way these things went. Sickness could not always be overcome, despite prayers. The memory of the sour rush of beer on her father's breath as he stamped past her on the stairs spoke of another way of coping.

After a few moments in front of Angela's stone she moved on. Another memorial caught her attention. Vandals must have attacked it, for the column of granite had been broken in two. Mrs Ellis bent down to make out the engraving on one of the four sides. "Resting place of Alfred Speedy, dearest husband of Rachel. Died 3 March 1867, aged 35. A light in our lives has gone out."

Maybe the dearest husband had died in an accident; the brick kilns and boat yards were not unused to crushing the bones and flesh of men. Had Rachel Speedy been left alone to raise a family? Mrs Ellis peered at the other sides of the memorial. They were blank—maybe there had been no money left at the end of Rachel's life to bury her with her husband. Or maybe she had decided to leave Auckland, to leave the place where the last of her husband's stringy remains lay fallow in the ground, and head south to the cold, or north to the missionaries, to begin again. Possibly—possibly she was *relieved* to be on her own. Maybe her husband beat her—many times—especially when drunk, beating out the unformed children in her belly, not caring if their only daughter watched from the bedroom doorway.

In the cemetery, Mrs Ellis pushed the memory away. It was better to wander, to tramp. She moved on, passing through the crumbling monuments to the earliest colonials. Families were buried together, siblings in adjoining plots, elderly couples within leeching distance as their bodies became one with the settling earth. Cemeteries are contradictory places, Mrs Ellis pondered, as she tried to focus upon the gravestones. Such memorials to temporality, to fleetingness; those that mourn erect stones to valorise a life passed too quickly. She thought that much was true of the collapsing pain of grief, when the heart seemed to fold in upon itself. She knew how the mother of baby Angela carried her sorrow. Each day of her daughter's life would be remembered and recalled; twisted by loss, the mother would invert the shortness of Angela's life by constantly picking at the threads of memory; reliving, re-feeling, even when—exhausted—she resisted. It was possible, Mrs Ellis accepted, that Angela's father felt the same.

And Rachel Speedy. Whether she had lived several years with Alfred or—like Mrs Ellis—had only a short time with a husband, grief, that concertina emotion, would cause the folding of their time together into small pockets of memory. Rachel would have no recollection of many weeks, even months, of their marriage; but she would remember the way Alfred laced his boots, or took his tea, or the smell of his skin after love. And now his grave, Angela's grave, was untended and overtaken by weeds and grass.

Mrs Ellis stood now at the top of the gully and in front

of the sallow marble slab marking the grave of Hobson, the old governor. There were no tussocks or vines creeping around this stone; someone must still tend to his plot. Such effort, Mrs Ellis wondered. It took a steely kind of courage to return to a grave and keep it clean and tidy.

The cemetery was silent, save for the odd call of a gull. No one had strayed amongst the dead today. And now Mrs Ellis was back out on Symonds Street, heading further into town. The vigour of the place, as ever, filled her with hope. Pedestrians and traps hummed about their business and, just up ahead, the white timber slats of Partington's windmill turned slowly in the stiffening air. Round and round they went: small circles of industry, grinding out the flour for another colonial breakfast.

Not that Mrs Ellis expected the residents of the large houses up ahead to eat such humble fare. Entering the homes of Auckland's wealthy on a charity mission was more daunting than stepping inside the shacks down at the harbour. Thankfully, some of the affluent were willing to give money to the cause, making the ordeal of crossing their hearths worthwhile.

Turning off Symonds Street and onto Wellesley Street East, Mrs Ellis approached the outskirts of Albert Park. This green addition to Auckland was new and she had yet to visit. She now watched the throng of contended strollers as they passed through iron gates to take the air. *I can understand their attraction to this place*, Mrs Ellis thought as she stepped onto the park's gravel path. The circular routes around the flower beds and the new, tiered bronze fountain at the park's centre, full of carp, seemed to exude a brazen confidence. Old stone barracks had previously occupied the land and were now completely cleared away. The talk was that things were settled with the Maoris; understandings had been reached, at least up here. So, now, not a brick or roof support was left of the fortress, once erected to protect the settlers. Mrs Ellis had a feeling that not all was as calm as it seemed; sometimes she saw the odd Māori trading at the dock, and couldn't help but wonder at their thoughts about the rapid changes their land had seen. Still. Albert Park had an air of freshness and Mrs Ellis breathed deeply.

Two women in fashionable black skirts and lace parasols vacated a bench nearby, so Mrs Ellis sat down, straightening out her dress self-consciously and tucking the patched places out of sight under her knees. The day had warmed up nicely, and the park was beginning to fill. Families walked together in groups, elderly gentlemen with smart canes swung by. Aucklanders were on the prowl, eager to take in the midday sun.

A brace of children ran past, shouting and chasing after a gull with a broken wing. They squealed as the bird flapped awkwardly, lumbering from side to side like a broken ship. A cry was on Mrs Ellis's lips, and she made to stand up—and then, thankfully, a park warden descended, rescuing the gull and ordering the children away.

Her eyes followed the warden as he disappeared into some bushes. After a few moments he reappeared, without the bird. Mrs Ellis was shocked, but understood. The

warden was doing the best he could. At least the end
would have been quick, and not drawn out. Not like the
babies in Onehunga … *but no, find something to focus
on, push that thought aside. There now, smile at the warden.* Mrs Ellis did so, wanly, as the park warden tipped
his cap in her direction, before striding away towards
the fountain.

A few moments later, a couple meandered by the
bench. The woman wore her hair high on her head, with
feathers inserted in the knot at various points in a care-
less but artful way. She laughed up at her companion
proprietarily, mouth and eyes wide as she claimed his
face. Taller than she, the man held her fingers, wrapped
around his upper arm. He wore a collar and a stylish
moustache. *Probably he works in an office—a lawyer
or customs officer,* Mrs Ellis considered. *They must be
engaged or newly-wed.* Something about this couple,
dancing by so confidently and with thoughts only of
each other, filled her with distaste. She was about to look
away when they stopped, quite close to her. The man
was reaching down to touch his woman's hair. A leaf had
blown in and was now caught in her tresses. Delicately,
tenderly, he removed it. Then, murmuring, he teased a
strand of blonde behind her ear, and—scandalously—
they kissed.

They walked on, oblivious to the woman sitting a few
feet away. Mrs Ellis watched them, chest hitching up and
down. She wondered if they were mocking her, if this
couple could see directly into her dry, empty body. But,
of course, they couldn't. They were lost to each other

and nothing else, nothing in the whole world, mattered a bit. Their tenderness for each other was overwhelming. *I remember feeling like that, twice in fact,* thought Mrs Ellis.

Even now, the past rose up at the most unexpected of moments. Not so long ago, memories came in a torrent, a swelling grief that stopped her breath and forced her into stillness. When that happened, Mrs Ellis could do nothing but wait for the chance to resurface, to rise up. It happened frequently on the passage out. Most of the other steerage passengers came to realise that she was a traveller carrying more than material belongings, and left her alone. One passenger did not, however; one morning, a woman with pale skin sat down next to her, uninvited. Mrs Ellis was holding her bible loosely and staring out at the horizon.

Quietly, in a nudging kind of way, the woman murmured in her ear. "You aren't reading that book at all."

Mrs Ellis shook her head but was unable to speak.

The woman eyed Mrs Ellis intensely. She had long brown hair, pinned back at the sides. Over on the poop deck, cabin passengers strolled the timber in their fine silks and hats. "You're just turning the pages, but you aren't reading. I can tell. My father is a cobbler but he taught me to read."

Mrs Ellis blinked.

The woman nodded softly. "Are you waiting for someone? Another passenger?" She blushed and glanced along their deck. "Me too. That's him—see?"

She twitched her head towards a thin man leaning

against a pile of sacking. His mouth was oddly curled, like a fish hook, and he moved his hands rapidly over his black hair, flattening and shaping. Mrs Ellis recalled her father, pacing the kitchen floor before wages day, marching and marching the eight steps from wall to wall.

"I'm not waiting for anyone," she said, desperately wanting this woman—more a girl—to go away.

"That's Oliver," the woman said and sighed happily. "I think he wants to marry me. Oh, isn't life wonderful?"

Mrs Ellis sat open-mouthed as the woman squeezed her arm before slipping over to the narrow man, his hands trembling as he embraced her. The women did not speak again throughout the rest of the crossing. Later, through a Good Templar, she heard that the woman had moved to Christchurch and lived in a boarding house. She did not know if Oliver went with her.

Agitated now, sitting on her bench in Albert Park, Mrs Ellis's hands fluttered, reaching out for the thing that, mostly, brought her comfort. She felt inside her pockets, searching—and, only then, she realised she had left her bible in the house at Onehunga.

The disquiet caused by such a loss was bright and acidic. The bible was a small, black, tattered thing, yet its absence was a brilliant red point; an unexpected, unwelcome punctuation point in the narrative of the day. A gift from a lifetime ago, filled with the names and dates of shadow-siblings and a husband and a child. It went everywhere with her as she marched for the Temperance cause. She had long since grown used to its delicate weight in her thin coat, bouncing comfortably against her thigh as she invaded the docks, the bars in the back streets and the bush farms with her message. And now it was lost.

Tears gathered at the edges of sight and, briefly, Mrs Ellis considered going back to Onehunga. But there was no money left for a dray and, if she were honest, no desire to trudge the five miles from the park. Legs, normally so strong and purposeful, were heavy and hot today. At the Good Templar Lodge, friends jokingly referred to her as "The Roamer"; they admired and puzzled at Mrs Ellis's ability to stroll around Auckland on her mission. She was, they said, a body of perpetual movement, always ready to go, always in motion. If only they knew. The tramping of Auckland's streets stretched the cord of remembrance. Small wooden crosses, resting silently under a dappled oak tree. A paced kitchen floor and an empty cradle. A man tying his bootlaces, smiling up at her. Yes. Her Good Templar friends would be surprised to see her sitting on this bench, all right.

The bible was probably still on Mrs Gray's kitchen table, the table where the child had been placed. The one baby Mrs Gray had decided to save. On her park bench, Mrs Ellis shuddered. The smell of the infant and its glassy, fixed stare had seeped through Mrs Ellis's very skin. After the discovery of the other children in the bedroom, she had taken the baby from Mrs Gray and walked to a neighbour, asking in a stammering, chattering voice for the police to be fetched. She had wondered, when away from Mrs Gray's house for those moments, if the woman would make a bolt for it. But she hadn't—Mrs Gray was swaying at the table when the constable arrived, her eyes drooping and an empty bottle at her elbow. She went with the quaking officer calmly enough. The baby, too, went to the police station so they, someone, could decide what to do with it. For a mad moment, Mrs Ellis had considered offering to take the child herself.

No, she couldn't go back to that house in Onehunga. She would just have to save up and buy another bible. The Lord would help her, though it might take a while to scratch together enough. Maybe a friend could lend her one in the meantime.

A yelp and the sound of a stumble brought her back to the park. Nearby, an elderly woman dressed in a short, tapered coat was bent over, rubbing her ankle. Standing close to her, one hand stroking the older woman's back soothingly, was a young girl, not long out of her teens. They wore matching sun hats. *Mother and daughter,* Mrs Ellis thought, *or maybe a grandmother and grandchild.* Related, certainly, and affectionate. She watched as they muttered together and the injured lady stood up slowly. She stretched out her back, and then her ankle. The women seemed to bunch up together, seeking and taking comfort from the warm proximity of their bodies. Then the older woman took an offered arm and moved on heavily. They made slow progress towards the park gates, and Mrs Ellis heard them laughing throatily as they went, their love for each other working out the day's kinks and strange twists of fate.

Such small moments of tenderness in this upside

down land, a little voice in Mrs Ellis's head said. What a place of hope and disappointment it is! What had Mrs Gray said earlier? That convention floats? That it travels along with you, hiding in the luggage and trunks of the displaced, ready to ensnare you? *Maybe*, thought Mrs Ellis, *but is not life what you make of it?* She had seen enough wealthy and titled settlers, brought low by drink, to believe that convention, class and respectability mattered little once temptation bit and a fortune had been passed across a bar. And the poor, those who had no money to waste in the first place—some found happiness and pleasure in the simplicity of domestic toil and a scratched kind of life. Convention, in the form of calling cards or tea parties, was unimportant to them, to the point of hilarity. No, here, in this colony, there are opportunities, but our hearts are the same; they are still pulled and crushed, still open to hope. Our flesh still yearns for the touch of someone long dead. We just go through it at the bottom of the world. Thank goodness God can still speak to us when we stand on our head.

There was relief in this type of rumination, and Mrs Ellis swirled around in such thoughts for a few moments. Then, with one eye on the women making their staggering way to the park's exit, she stood up. The Lodge was not far from here; if she walked steadily, she could be in time for afternoon tea. A scalding hot cup of tea and maybe a sliver of fruit cake. A fondness for sweet things was a forgivable weakness, she decided, rubbing her fingertips together. She flicked away the image of the smashed iced birthday cake at Mrs Gray's house, and fixed her mind on a simpler, sturdier, more *honest* kind of indulgence. Yes. That was what she would do. She would brush the memories of today into a pile, not to be disturbed, and would drink deeply from a cracked china cup. Small, tender moments. That was the way forward for Mrs Ellis. She strode forward, slapping her hand on her thigh as her empty pockets bounced.

Dressed for the Funeral

The house was on Auckland's Lorne Street, near the new park; it muscled out into the road, shouldering its bricked presence upon a street populated with wooden buildings. The neighbouring houses seemed to sit back, cowed by the red stone and shaped lintels. Arched windows of coloured, rolled plate glass glittered imperfectly in the midday sun as mourners gathered; some threaded their feet over the blue, yellow and red glints of light thrown onto the dust.

It was not a long walk from their rooms on Union Street, but George needed a cupped elbow to assist him as they rounded Abercrombie for the last push, and by the time they joined the other mourners he was breathing hard. He borrowed Pip's handkerchief to mop his brow. Bringing the cotton square trimmed with black up to her own flushed face, she tasted his salt.

Soft murmurs united those outside the house. They were dressed in black; the women in light crepe and the men suffering under the weight of dress coats. Pip turned around to look, to count, conscious of George leaning against her and the speed of his breath. Maybe forty or so. Who knew there were so many of them, in this young city? Tucked away in their narrow box, cut off, it seemed, from life—she had thought there was just the two of them with their kind of dreams. Or, these days, just George, scratching away on sheets of thin paper, bundling them up at the end of every day and sending Pip on an errand to the dock.

George wheezed and his old bones formed a claw around the flesh above her elbow. "A good show. Ellen would have been pleased."

Pip squinted at the house; curtains drawn on the second floor, roses pruned back. A man with a fixed, solemn expression stood outside the closed door. "How well did you know her?"

"As well as any writer in this city." George coughed and lowered his eyes. Pip was reminded of the way he greeted their landlord. "She was much revered."

"Oh?"

George pressed his fingers into the soft meat of her upper arm. "*The Revolt of Isabelle*? *Sweetly on the Wind*? That was Ellen."

"I have not read ..."

"We will add them to the list."

Pip looked away. It was difficult to control her splintering thoughts. George had been speaking in such a manner, in his heavy attempt to educate her, from the moment they left the church last week. She supposed it was because she was, finally, legally his, for him to shape. He had many instructions. She was not to fiddle with the ring; it would draw attention and questions. Better to allow their news to slip easily into the conversation, like milk in tea. She should pack away the tiny vests and shawls—what did she keep them for anyway? Too painful to have them around, and she might begin to weep. George would prefer she did not do that. Likewise, he would prefer if she did not cry during their private moments. He was not especially rough—age had taught him *some* things and, besides, there was his leg—and he was taking what was only his by right. Pip scuffed the dancing colours on the street, thrown down by the mottled windows. She wondered if resentment had a natural hue. As an emerald block wove persistently amongst the mourner's feet, she decided it did.

A tall man with a red cravat and top hat drawn straight, it seemed, from the pages of a Paris weekly (though George's were several years out of date) appeared at their side and struck up a murmuring conversation. George turned at once and Pip was released. She rubbed her arm absently, listening to George's gulping chatter; it was as though he were sucking the man's words into his body. She drifted to the fence running parallel to the house and took off a glove, grasping the cool iron.

"I wondered if you would be here." A man stood in front of her. Slim and blonde, he cast her in narrow shadow, peering down over thin-rimmed spectacles, whiskers on long cheeks.

Behind him, George was deeply entwined in polite conversation. She could tell from the rise and fall of his hands how he enjoyed it, how he glided on it.

"It must have been, oh, six months? How are you?" The man's voice fell softly in the space between them. At that moment they occupied a hot vacuum. Beyond, on the shimmering road, the mourners looked, to Pip, like smudged columns of chalk.

Pip blinked and cleared her throat. "I am well, thank you."

"Good. Did you know Ellen Bradbury? I did not realise."

"No, no." *I am no use at this*, Pip thought desperately. *I've forgotten how to talk to him.*

"It is good to see you, Philippa. Are you—is she with you?" The man plucked at his coat sleeves, tugging them down past his wrists. His bottom lip twisted up into his moustache. "I don't expect you would bring her to a funeral. Who is caring for her?"

"I'm here with someone." Pip was aware her voice was shrill and jagged. The crowd on the street were not so far away. She cast around for George, aware of her new need for him, and bitter at the fact.

The man opened his mouth a little. "Oh."

"My husband. Mr Arnold." Pip nodded quickly in George's direction.

The man swivelled his head between Pip and the old man over his shoulder. Back and forth, darting like a bird. And then the man seemed to sag forward, his frame losing all rigidity. Pip wondered if he might puddle at her feet. His jaw rolled and rocked, and a gasping sound burst forth. And then another, a strangled yelp. Figures of chalk turned round to see, to frown, and the man brought a shaking handkerchief to his lips. There were tears in his eyes.

"Stop it!" Pip trembled. "I beg, Luke, do not embarrass me."

"I'm sorry." The man, Luke, rubbed the cloth across his face. His cheeks wobbled in the heat. "But Philippa— George Arnold? I can't believe it. Did you forget his articles?"

"No." Faintly, reluctantly.

"His ridiculous passages about the majestic bush and the freedom of the flats. It used to drive you wild."

Pip remembered. Wet Tauranga afternoons a life time ago, the pair of them creeping around the print rooms as her father's paper went to press. After school, before school; meeting outside the building on Durham Street, sneaking past old Mr Henry overseeing the churning white sheets. An acrid smell in their noses, tasting it on their tongues. They loved the fever of print days, the hullabaloo of words, ideas, captured on a page. Although he pretended not to see them, Mr Henry took to leaving a fresh copy on the office table, sometimes next to a jug of warm milk. Pip and Luke never tired of craning over the wet pages, heads close together, white moustaches on their lips.

They became critics. For weeks one summer, they tore into George's missives from his walking tour; Pip would jab at the damp ink, a black fingertip marking out her disdain for someone trying to frame her country in a few hundred words. "Who is he writing *for*?" she had spluttered—she remembered *that*. His garbled mix of nightingales and keas—of course their calls didn't sound the same!—and the comparison between English ferns and speargrass. How ridiculous! Pip would shout, and grind her teeth against the idiocy of the tourist. She and Luke even tried to intercept George's posted article on one occasion and amend it before it reached Pip's father; John Hagger, though, knew his daughter's writing well enough to deliver his punishment—cleaning the type-face after their lessons—with suppressed amusement.

Now, George spoke of another tour, taking Pip with him this time. Somewhere north, near the missionaries. Near the Maoris, even; he had a hankering to bracket their brown skin within a tidy hundred words or so. Pip closed her eyes briefly and swayed next to the iron fence. She thought of the dried bundles George gave to her most evenings, bound with string. The master at the quayside was always pleased to see her and feel the press of a coin. "George—he—I send new articles to his agent almost every day."

"There was once a time when you would have hoped that his agent used them to line his boots or kindle his fire." Luke stared blearily at the thin band on Pip's hand. "Why? When did you give up?"

A whip of sting in those words. Pip swallowed them, feeling them burn into her gums. She wanted to tell him everything, to wipe away his questions with her spit. Her arms ached with an absence of which she could not speak, the flesh on her ankles craved the brush of sticky fat fingers. But then George blundered back into view and stood beside her. His white head scuffed her shoulder.

"My dear?" he warbled, warm with talk.

After a week, she had become used to the expectation in his voice. "What will you wear?" he had asked the morning Ellen Bradbury's death was announced, as they shared a slice of bread. Underneath the question, of course, was an instruction. So she dyed a precious blouse black, pinning back her enmity with the folded cotton. George had laid his outfit out on their bed from the moment he saw the death notice. For two days, between the appearance of brief lines in the paper and the funeral, he floated about their rooms with taut excitement. "There will be many artists of importance at the funeral," he advised. "Anyone who is anyone in Auckland will show up." Pip stood in the doorway between the sitting room and small kitchen, watching her new husband dance his way around his thoughts. He had never been so unrestrained.

Now George looked at Luke curiously. Caught, Pip could do nothing.

"George, this is Mr Luke Woods. He's an old friend from Tauranga, and a writer; I believe Warnes of London has published his latest work."

Luke wiped his face for the last time and tucked the handkerchief into his coat pocket. He was quite composed; Pip recognised the way his eyelids drooped as he regained control. As a boy, Luke had been unable to look at her directly when suppressing a thought or feeling—only once had he stared directly at her and spoken without restraint. "Thank you, Philippa. You are kind; the notice in the *Observer* was quite small."

"An accomplishment, though." George's voice was brittle. He extended thin fingers, allowing for the briefest of shakes.

"Yes, I was surprised at the reception. *Pall Mall* gave it an excellent write up."

The two men stood apart, the air between them bright and ripe. George rubbed his fingers together in a small circle, soothing his flesh the way he might if blanched by nettles. The movement made a soft sound, like sand on stone; Pip squeezed her eyes shut, thinking of an evening at the bay and warm, dimpled flesh.

George opened and closed his mouth, on the verge of speech. Then he turned back to Pip. "We should talk to the Chadwicks, Philippa. Archibald has an agent he wants to recommend. Agents, eh, Woods?" he flicked his head, and Pip watched as he formed a rueful smile. "Either conduits or hindrances to success."

"Indeed," Luke muttered blandly and, as they walked away into the throng of mourners, Pip knew her old friend was shaking his head. She looked over her shoulder at the man from her past, who was studying the coloured lights at his feet. A ghost living beneath her skin wanted to slip free and go to him, to be that girl he remembered; to sit on the rickety wharf at Tauranga and skip stones across the bay, to stand outside the booksellers on the Strand and imagine their own novels on sale, to throw off the straw bonnets of school and sit in Elms Park and daydream about leaving for Auckland.

But she felt so weak these days—her other, present self would disappear if the Pip of the past suddenly reared up and went to Luke. There was no space in her body for two people, not any more. So she allowed George to relocate her, to place her in the centre of the shrouded figures, who murmured as they closed around the new-comers like a sea. And here was Archibald Chadwick, looking like a sand flounder with his squashed face and flattened chin. A man she had never met before, he introduced himself like an old friend, pushing his wife forwards—make acquaintance, make acquaintance. Pip smiled, rocks in her mouth. How could she talk to him, when she could not find the words for Luke? She wanted to run but the mourners, the group, was glutinous and held her still. They stood against a bleached sky, only the turning circle of Partington's windmill breaking the horizon. Pip plucked at her high collar, conscious of the heat, the heat.

"Not long, dear," Mrs Chadwick leaned in, kind-ness creasing her expansive face. "We will be leaving for Symonds Street shortly. Ellen always wanted to be buried at midnight, I've heard—something about the doorway between night and day. Her nephew decided that would not be proper, so settled on a noon funeral instead."

"Oh?"

"You look pale." Mrs Chadwick pushed Pip's hair from her forehead with a maternal ease. "I hear you are recently married?"

Ah, a question beneath a question. Pip was devel-oping an ear for these things, though was not yet sure how to answer. "George is old, Mrs Chadwick. We are not—that is, we are not looking to become parents." The words were out before she knew it, bald and blazing.

Mrs Chadwick, experienced and round of chest, puffed up with amusement, and patted Pip on the arm. "Do not close the door too early. Children bring unexpected joy."

Pip looked at the place Mrs Chadwick had laid her warm hand. "Yes. They do."

"Besides, I hear you are something of a writer?"

"Do you?" What more surprises would this day hold? "I haven't been a writer for some time."

Mrs Chadwick looped her arms beneath her hefty bosom. "Wasn't there a children's book a year or so ago? Colonial fairy tales, that's it. George is very proud of you, mentions it all the time."

"Does he?" Pip shifted uneasily, wishing she could sit.

"George says they were very good if a little—what was the word?—*parochial*." Mrs Chadwick nodded for emphasis.

"Does he?" Pip repeated. She looked at her husband, in bowed conversation with Archibald Chadwick. The hems of his trousers were a little frayed, a little scuffed from the street. "Well, I no longer write fairy tales, Mrs Chadwick."

"No?" though she was not really interested, Pip could tell.

"I stopped believing."

"I beg your pardon?" The stout lady drew herself up. Anxiety closed like a curtain; Pip was willing to bet Mrs Chadwick had not imagined the conversation would have gone like this. Much better to be bland and taste-less, and easy to digest. The older woman cast about, glancing up and down, her fingers following the string of pearls at her throat, hoping for other, safer conversation.

Her hook hit home; two women talking nearby threw out their words like life rafts, drawing a grateful Mrs Chadwick in.

"Did you hear the news? It was in the *Observer* a few days ago."

"No?" A breathy rush from Mrs Chadwick. "What news?"

The women repositioned themselves, moving closer. Pip was aware of their faint lavender scent, their shared noses and brows; sisters, most likely.

"A house at Onehunga. A constable found the bodies of two babies in a room upstairs, and more in the gar-den." One sister beamed importantly.

Listening, air caught in Pip's throat. Something odd happened to her chest—there was a leak. Heat was leak-ing out into her lungs and breasts, pooling beneath her skin. Her whole body seemed to open up, to melt out-wards as she strained to hear the next words. What was coming, what house?

"Someone from the Temperance Society found them," the younger sister babbled. "The woman living there had been taking babies in and drugging them. Seems she had been doing it for years."

"What babies?" Pip whispered.

"All kinds, dearie," the older sister said cheerfully. "Wicked women who no longer wanted their children.

Children from poor families. *Unmarrieds.*"

"Where was this? Where was the house?" Pip was aware of Mrs Chadwick's glance.

"I think it was—Cameron Street, yes. In Onehunga." The sisters bobbed together, little corks of certainty. "The paper said it was quite a respectable looking house from the outside. The woman obviously had money. I imagine that some mothers sent cheques on a regular basis, maybe really believing their child was alive and cared for. The Temperance lady found her sitting on the kitchen floor with one child, still alive."

A fizzy sort of cloud descended upon Pip at that moment. It forced her shoulders to sink in, her knees to lock together. There was a crackle in her ears and she tasted bile, like sherbet, in her throat. Her teeth clamped down fiercely on her tongue. The ground became soft and pliable beneath her feet, and sweat broke through the skin on her brow.

"I am feeling …"

"Mrs Arnold? Is it the heat?" Mrs Chadwick rubbed her ample bosom against her, placing a splayed hand in the middle of Pip's back.

"No. Yes." A shaking hand to her head. A snapped look from side to side. Figures surrounded her, but all Pip could really see was a carpet bag, full of bonnets and smocks.

"She's a newly-wed, you know." Mrs Chadwick steered her up towards the house.

"Ah," said the spinster sisters, pretending to understand.

"I need to find Luke …"

"You mean George. The heat really has got to you, hasn't it?"

"No, Luke!"

"Now, don't take on. We'll get you inside. I'll let George know you aren't feeling well." Mrs Chadwick had doughy strength in her fat arms. Her breasts, firm as oranges, were cushioned against Pip's side as she steered a path through black figures. "This way, my sweet. One foot in front of the other."

The firm hand on her back took Pip back to being a child again. Her mother was forcing her up the stairs to bed, to sleep off the fever of chicken pox. She was not to play with Luke, not to race around the park like a crazy animal; she was to take a cool bath and lie down, until the white, raised bumps on her skin gave way to blisters. Her mother's soft, sweet face drifted on the Auckland haze and Pip gave up. She allowed Mrs Chadwick to propel her forward while other images came at her from all directions. Pip put out a hand, as though trying to wave them away, or reorder them. A corset of pain around her stomach, a desire to push, calling out for an absent, long-dead mother, and then a wet bundle in her arms. White teeth breaking through pink gums, a rounded cheek. Laughing over a soft-boiled egg on a Sunday morning. Half-ideas, words scribbled on paper, unfinished and screwed up. Her fountain pen atop a stack of folded napkins, bleeding out blue ink. George. A last glance at a closing door, the child in another woman's arms.

Her knees gave way, and Mrs Chadwick was under her, forcing her to stand. The older woman exhaled hoarsely, but she was able to drag them both up the stairs to the house on Lorne Street.

"A lady needs to sit down," she barked at the silent man outside the front door, and Pip heard her mutter something about mutes and funeral costs. So that was who the serious-looking man was—a mute, a mourner paid by the undertakers to stand and look grief-stricken. *What a wasteful expense*, Pip thought. *We barely have enough to eat.*

The air inside the house was much cooler. Squinting, Pip took in the drapes over picture frames and mirrors. They were in a small parlour. A clock on the mantelpiece had been stopped.

"You lie there," Mrs Chadwick commanded and forced Pip down onto a sofa. "Feet up." She adjusted a firm pillow behind Pip's head. "When did you last have a monthly visit?"

"What? Oh, Mrs Chadwick, I told you, George and I—" Pip closed her eyes, not wanting to talk about George's methods.

"Nonsense." Mrs Chadwick stood up, her frame looming above Pip. "That's probably what's at the root of this, even if you've been married just a week. He is a man after all. Lie here please, and I'll see about getting you some water."

She disappeared through a side door and Pip heard her thumping steps, fainter, disappearing. She took a shaky breath and sat up.

The room was dark and had an unpleasant, musty smell. Even the chandelier and table lamps had been covered with cloth. Not a piece of colourful material was on display; all had been sanitised, made mournful. Pip bit her lip. Her father had not been as excessive when his wife had died. He asked Pip to stop the clock in the dining room, where Martha was to be laid out, and Pip had taken down the paper butterflies she had pinned to the ceiling above her mother's sick bed; but the house carried on as normal. John Hagger had even arranged for the funeral to be held on a Sunday, so not to interrupt the Saturday print run.

I cannot imagine Ellen Bradbury's family would miss her any more than I miss my mother, Pip thought. George had told her that Ellen had only one nephew and no children of her own, and he lived in Wellington. He is hardly likely to cover the paintings and mirrors because he is broken-hearted, Pip decided. And, irrationally but unavoidably, she resented the unnamed nephew for his artifice and pretence.

She stood up. Blood flooded back into her feet and she padded up and down, fighting cramp. The room was an odd shape, long and thin. An oak sideboard stretched down one side, and to Pip's right stood a small table. A covered lamp sat upon it. Absently, Pip peeled back the drape, exposing a delicate glass shade—a beautiful purple colour. A box of matches lay nearby, and she lit the oil in the lamp. She dropped the drape on the sofa and stood up, carrying the lamp over to the paintings on the wall.

She pulled the covers away and, one by one, they were exposed. A seascape, possibly a steamer on Auckland harbour; a collection of flowers in a vase, English meadow-types that Pip recognised from her mother's books back in Tauranga; a Māori hut, with a group of brown men talking to white missionaries, pointing to a book. Obviously the bible. Pip stood back, regarding her discoveries. *An odd juxtaposition of images,* she thought— *old and new worlds hung side by side.*

"I painted some and bought the others." A voice to her left.

Pip looked round. The light from the purple lamp seemed to double everything up, to blur the edges. Pip could not make out who had spoken, and then she saw.

The object she had thought was a sideboard was, in fact, not a sideboard. Someone was lying in it—*had* been lying in it—and was now sitting up. A woman. White hair pinned up into a bun, a tight lace collar at her neck. Her cheeks were rouged and shiny.

"Yes, painted that one of a *pā,*" the woman said. "Went on a trek into the bush back—oh, must have been the '50s. My sister thought I was mad. It's all the rage now, isn't it? Walking tours."

"Ellen Bradbury," Pip said flatly. It was a statement, not a question. She was certain that she spoke to the writer, the revered lady of letters, whose funeral she now attended.

"That's right," and the woman's head rattled alarmingly on her neck. She put a hand up to her temple to still it. The flesh on her hands was also shiny, like marble. "Excuse me. I keep forgetting that they cut my throat open to insert a breathing tube, right at the end. It didn't help, of course."

"No." Pip passed the lamp between her hands. She was not the least bit afraid. In fact, she felt slightly giddy, as though she might burst into laughter.

"There's port under that table," and Ellen Bradbury pointed at the table next to the sofa. "My nephew doesn't know about it, or else he would have helped himself."

"Thank you. I would be glad of a glass." Pip retreated to the sofa and sat back down, returning the lamp to the table. She wondered how Ellen knew she needed a drink. Can she read my thoughts?

"Of course I can," Ellen said. "You don't think I'm really sitting up talking to you, do you? I'm as dead as anything. But Dottie isn't."

Pip paused, her fingertips scraping the cold bottle tucked away under the table. "What do you know about Dottie?"

"Nothing." Ellen Bradbury grinned. "Or everything, depending on your religion. I know that you tried very hard not to love her. It was only an experiment with Luke, wasn't it? That night at the bay? You wanted to see how far you could let him go before backing out, before demanding he regain control. But neither of you could. You weren't expecting it to feel the way it did."

"Like being where we needed to be," Pip murmured. Suddenly she was back, sitting on the wharf with Luke as the orange sun flattened into the water. He held her hand—she let him, on this last night before leaving for Auckland—and when the harbour-master came round on his inspections he pulled Pip away, towards the bush beyond the streets. They had lain together near the twisted trunk of a rata tree, and he said he loved her. He had not looked away and Pip, to her surprise, had met his gaze. When it was over and the desire of years was wet against their skin, Pip left. No last words or kisses; just a small glance backwards as she walked back home to pack and leave. She took a red flower from the tree trunk and held it in her fist; the following day, in Auckland, when she was shown to her room in the home of her father's friend, she placed the flower between the pages of a book.

"That's right." Ellen smiled, exposing brown stumps instead of teeth. "You wanted him all that time and didn't know it. And when you realised, it was too late to stop. You didn't even want to. Poor Luke, with his thin chest and hairless arms. He's different now, isn't he? What a man. George isn't a patch on him. Are you going to drink that?" Ellen extended a ringed finger to the bottle in Pip's hand. "Take a drink, I shan't mind."

Pip brought the port to her lips and slowly sipped from the bottle. Her eyes did not leave the woman's face.

"That night at the bay was the last time you were together before you left for Auckland, wasn't it?" Ellen ran her tongue over her lips, glaring at the port. "You knew he would follow you, when you wrote and told him. What a letter it must have been for him to read—your book of stories was going to be published, and he was about to become a father. What about your own father? Did you expect him to forgive you?"

Pip bowed her head. "Oh, I hoped—" John Hagger had cabled once Pip's disgrace became apparent. Of course, she could no longer stay in the home of his friend and his wife, and their children must be protected. They had given her a home on trust, a place of safety while she wrote her stories and tried to make something of the writing business, and this was how she repaid them. It was something, at least, that her mother was dead. It was up to Pip what she now did with her small inheritance, and Hagger enclosed details of an account. She was not to contact him again, even if the child died.

"But you wanted the baby to die anyway, didn't you Pip?" Ellen rolled her hands together, the sound rough and dry. "You wanted it to bleed out of you or die without its first breath. I'm sorry to speak so harshly, but that's how you felt. Regardless of what your father thought, a baby and a career do not go together. Look, I understand *that*, believe me. Why do you think I never married? Someone wanted me, soon after I landed here. A man from Wellington. I even loved him for a while. But you cannot write, cannot live as an artist, when a child is present. George recognised that too, didn't he, and made it a condition of your marriage?"

"He did." Pip thought of George staring at Dottie as she played on the floor of Pip's single room when he came to court her, and the careful way he decided she had to be sent away.

"So you didn't want to marry Luke, you didn't want to have his child, you didn't want to love Dottie—but you did. When she arrived, after all those hours and all that pain, you could not help but love her plumpness. Her round, grabbing hands."

"Her appetite."

"Oh, yes!" Ellen threw back her head and laughed. Pip saw the blood on her collar. "She could eat, couldn't she?" Ellen hiccuped. "You'd never known a baby to demand so much milk. Your breasts were red raw."

"I didn't mind." But it was more than that. Pip revelled in it. She took pride in the pull of her flesh. Most days it seemed worthwhile. On yellow mornings, when Dottie ate her Sunday egg and the curve of her cheek bounced as she chewed, poverty and rinsed grey shoes were unimportant.

"No, you didn't. Little Dottie, little Dot, your little mistake. She was the love of your life, Pip-squeak, no matter how hard you tried to make her small and unimportant. Luke only saw her at a month old before you sent him away. He offered to take her back to Tauranga, to his mother—alarm bells should have rung then, my dear. You couldn't bear to be parted with her."

"No, I could not." And, suddenly, the lightness of her arms and the absence of Dottie's warmth against her chest became overwhelming. Pip dropped the bottle of port and clenched her hands together, bringing them inwards. She leaned over, buckling forward over a body, a baby, who was not there. She thought of the flower, the rata flower brought to Auckland and preserved in the pages of a book. A wet, wide mouth, a burst of life. Pip wept.

"Tears. I remember those." Ellen sniffed. "Some people thought me cold and unfeeling—all to do with never having a husband, you see? But I put all those feelings in my books. As you want to, don't you Pip? You want to write about this place of your birth with honesty, not the tourist drivel that George writes and is swallowed up by ignorant new chums fresh off the boat." Ellen stroked her throat. "There is always a cost. You can't do all that and be the kind of writer you want without exploring and experiencing. And you can't do that without money and connections. And you can't make those connections and earn that money with a child."

Pip eased her shaking body against the sofa. The chair was firm and reassuring, and she leaned against it, pressing her flesh backwards as she struggled for control. Tears were caught in her handkerchief, still damp from George's brow, and she was careful not to bring it to her lips again.

"What do you think I should do?" She would never have asked that question, once upon a time. But things were so different now, her spirit broken into Dottie-sized pieces.

Ellen seemed delighted to have been asked. "Yes, that question remains, doesn't it? Should you tell Luke? He could find her. It was only a few days ago; Dottie might not be one of those bodies in the bedroom or the garden. She might be the baby left alive. Luke could go out to Onehunga and find out. He would be angry that you'd sent her out to be cared for, but finding her alive is the most important thing, isn't it?"

"Yes." Pip sniffed.

"He might still want you, after all this. He would understand, eventually, that desperation drove you to George—that and his meagre connections to other writers."

"He might—we might …"

"Of course, you are thinking what other options there are." Ellen grinned widely, once again baring her discoloured teeth. "It's only natural, for someone like you. Like *me*. Well, you could do *nothing*. Nothing at all. You could go to my funeral and go home with George. You could write to Luke in a few months and tell him Dottie has died. She might already be dead, after all. And you could start writing again. You could go on that walking tour with George and see what becomes of it. You could write the books this country is crying out to read—nothing like my angry books with a purpose, arguing for the vote and sensible dress. Your books could be about life, real life out here, and what the land means—or doesn't mean. You just have to decide what's more important to you. Men get to have everything, you see, and women don't. They have to make a choice."

At that moment the door opened. Pip gasped and sat up, snapping her head round to Ellen. But Ellen was not there. Instead, a corpse lay in the coffin, peaceful and serene, lace at her throat and her hands clasped tightly together. The woman's hair was tidy and pinned back, her lips firmly shut. Pip shook her head, bewildered. She rubbed her temples.

"Here, water." Mrs Chadwick bustled forward with a glass. She handed it to Pip, her foot catching on the port bottle rolling and slopping onto the carpet. "What's this?" She stooped to pick it up. "Oh no, dear, you don't want that. You'd only feel worse. Sip some water, there now."

Pip bent over the glass and drank. She squeezed her eyes shut. Had Ellen really been there, talking to her? Or was she going mad? Was the heat or grief sending her over the edge?

Mrs Chadwick sat down heavily next to her on the sofa. "There now, feeling better?"

"A little."

"Good." Mrs Chadwick took the glass from her. "We should be leaving for the cemetery shortly. I've spoken to George, and you can stay here, if you like. Rest up."

"No, I think—"

"And, did you ask me to find Luke?" Mrs Chadwick patted Pip's knee. "When I brought you up to the house, out of the sun? It's just that there is a Luke here. George was talking to him. Seems he knows you."

Pip leaned against Mrs Chadwick. "I can't remember."

"Well, have a little think." Mrs Chadwick stood up slowly. Her over-worked thighs trembled under her dress and she shuffled for balance. "I'm going to take this back to the kitchen. When I come back, let me know who you want me to fetch, if anyone. Luke or George."

She smiled and stroked Pip's stained cheek, and then turned away. She left the door open and Pip, lying back down again, listened to her skirts swish away down the corridor. Outside she heard the crowd gathering, preparing for the next move. She shook her head, trying to think, to decide what to do for the best.

INK AND RED LACE

Oddly, the first thing she noticed was the paper. Thick, sponge-like to the touch, cushioning the press of fingers—where could Laura have got it from? They hadn't been in Christchurch for over a year, but the paper was obviously shop-bought and expensive. How could she have come by it, so far out here on the Plains? Could she have bought it on their last visit to town and hidden it away all this time? It was possible. The cost wouldn't have been insurmountable.

Frances considered. Laura had sold a bundle of lace ribbons to a few stores and a couple of Māori traders, and been shyly pleased with her takings. *They were well deserved*, her mother thought, for Laura had worked all winter with a feather cushion on her knee, bobbins flying in the fading light, creating red, blue, white ribbons from odd bits of thread. The traders liked intricate braiding, Laura had said, returning from the Māoris' with a coy smile on her face. The style of the ribbons was a little too modern for Frances's tastes, and she preferred simpler, easier patterns. In a moment of honesty, she admitted to her daughter that she had not the patience to work with such detail. Also, she especially disliked the red sashes. The colour seemed impertinent. Frances wondered what sort of woman would wear them. But the last four years had taught her not to worry about such things, and to make money where she could. Besides, Laura said, red was popular, and she had been asked to bring some more on her next visit to town. So yes, maybe Laura *had* slipped away and bought the artist pad with her modest purse. Possibly the watercolours, too, and charcoal. And she had hidden them, somewhere, in this little house.

Frances smoothed out the pages on the small table, letting sunshine from the one window fall across the surface. With its low ceiling, the kitchen felt like a pressed cube of space, and Frances fought a constant battle to draw light into the room. Over the years Hans had resisted putting in another window simply, Frances suspected, because she wanted one so much. So Frances made subtle compromises where she could. Clothes were not allowed to dry inside and add their heavy shade to the room; even in winter, skirts and work shirts were kept out on the run, where sheep occasionally nudged their interest. On cold mornings, Laura and Annabelle had to stand outside, shivering, and flap movement into rigid dresses. Their thin arms would pump the fabric enthusiastically, like bellows breathing life into an old woman. And the old settler trick of papering walls with newspapers was also rejected, in case it seemed to make the walls pile up on the inhabitants; instead, Frances painted the timbers white and ignored the chill creeping through the gaps in the slats.

The added benefit was that the kitchen was cool, even during the summer. For this, Frances was grateful. She had once been in the Sanderson house, up at the Station, to welcome William's new wife. The warmth of their homestead had nearly choked her. Always the dramatist, Hans had sneered when she'd mentioned it on their walk home. So damned embarrassing.

She wondered what he would make of this discovery, of the papers she had found under the narrow mattress Laura and Annabelle shared. He would probably say something cruel and unnecessary. He would goad Laura, poking and probing with well-placed words until he found tears. Hans was like a water-diviner, seeking out moisture beneath a taut surface.

These drawings had to belong to Laura. At nine, Annabelle was too young. True, some of the figures were nothing more than stickmen, but the perspective was just right and the trick of drawing the viewer into the centre of the piece was unnervingly good. Frances traced the edges of the paper with her fingertips. The scene must have been painted near to the house—how had Laura managed to do it unnoticed? An uncomfortable sensation nudged at Frances's breastbone; this morning's discoveries seemed to push Laura to the edge of sight, out to the periphery of her mother's domain. It was because the painting was so *good*. It was of a small watering hole amidst a yellow-brown expanse of scrubland. Laura had sketched the Southern Alps in the distance, colouring the rocks just the right kind of blue against the lurid sky. Jagged peaks of differing sizes stretched from left to right across the canvas, and white clouds rose above them. Frances shook her head. She could not resist—she touched the small figures beside the watering hole, who appeared to be setting up camp. They seemed so fragile yet sturdy, and her eye was drawn to them.

The second painting was of a similar size but more focused. Three merino sheep grazed amongst the tussocks and, staring down at the table, the intricacy of this piece made Frances shake. Every blade of burnished grass seemed to have been painted individually; the delicate weave of the merino wool shone out, the spikes of the speargrass appeared so sharp Frances figured they might cut her. Ever the dramatist, Hans whispered in her mind, and she tried to swallow the resentment in her throat. *But these are outstanding*, she thought, unable to deny the fact. *Oh Laura.*

Frances sat down slowly on a stool. Of course, she could guess why Laura had kept it secret; four years of living with Hans had made them all skittish and private. But over the past year or so, soon after turning fourteen, Laura had been especially wary. Perhaps, Frances believed, it was because, of the three of them, Laura had the clearest memory of life before Hans entered their family in his bullish way. Laura remembered Linwood. Annabelle had only those milky, infant reminiscences of a father's caress, and Frances had squashed the past down into a secret place, hoping for a clean start with a new husband. But Laura, eight when Linwood died, had her memories: sitting on his knee at the piano, rubbing his feet by the fire, helping him set out the bibles on a Sunday. Now, she seemed to carry her sorrow at her father's early death in the curve of her body. Her back bent that little more, her chin rested on her chest for longer. She developed a habit of squeezing her eyes shut when Hans blundered about in one of his rages; a habit that edged his fury further and made her a target.

But such assertiveness in her painting! And Frances touched the drawings again. Her quiet little girl, with her relentless eye for detail, had found something to sustain her in this land, this land she had been brought to without consultation as a young child. Well. Something had to be done about this precocious talent. That was all there was for it, as Linwood would say.

"I didn't expect you to find them." A small murmur from the open door, and Laura appeared. Her face was pinched and pale as she entered the room. In her hands she held a bundle of leafy stalks, beaded with red berries. She set them down on the table, over the paintings.

"Laura. These are wonderful."

"Has he seen them?"

"No!" Frances glanced over her daughter's shoulder, to the small block of daylight through the kitchen door. She strained to see Hans's form, to glimpse his thin body. "Where is he?"

"At the boundary hut at the edge of the run. He said he wanted to check for sheep that had missed the muster."

Frances nodded slowly. "Sanderson must be in a fix if he wants them all sheared. He's always at the bank, Hans says."

Laura drew up a stool and sat opposite her mother. "Was that what he was raging about yesterday? Annabelle heard him—something about his wages?"

Frances winced, knowing how easily her youngest became frightened. "Hans hasn't been paid for nearly a month. That would infuriate any man."

Laura looked away at the pleading note that came into her mother's voice. A telling silence swelled between them. Frances shifted on her stool, and patted the drawings.

Laura transferred her gaze down and coyly asked, "Do you like them?"

Frances longed to reach out to her. She's still my girl, still my girl, her heart sang, and she wanted to heap parental approval upon Laura, banking it up around her like a shelter against the world. Instead, she said, "They are beautiful," wishing she could say something to convey the pleasure the drawings had given her. Linwood had always been the talker.

But, it was enough. Laura turned pink and plaited her legs together. "I thought Hans would be angry at my wasting money. On paper and paints. That's why I hid them."

Oh, but Hans really had wormed his way into the fabric of their thoughts! Frances pursed her lips. It was true—he would have been angry. She glanced at the day old mutton leeching grease into her one good saucepan, the stale bread used at breakfast time, and felt as though she were seeing them for the first time. The frayed edges of her cuffs brushed the table as she reached for Laura's hand.

"Perhaps we can keep them tucked away. You know, until there's a good time to show him." She was whispering, drawing her daughter in. Drawing her in to what, Frances was not sure. Hans seemed to linger in the background like a shadow.

Laura shrugged. "He would hate them anyway. Sometimes I think he detests me, except when…" She broke off and bit her lip. Shutters seemed to come down over her eyes. "Well, I hardly see him now, except when he comes in to eat, or drink all that tea. If he's not on the run he's at the Sanderson's place." She smiled suddenly. "Do you know, I think Mrs Sanderson is going to have a baby? Her belly looked round when I took her some butter on Saturday."

This last was said quickly, with no thought. Frances smiled as well, though news like this always caused a pain that could not be pushed away. The barrenness of her ageing body shamed her and had infuriated Hans. "It's possible. They have been married for a while, after all. And Mrs Sanderson is young." Almost a girl, she wanted to say, and plucked at the loose skin on the back of her hands. She nodded down at the paintings again. Light fell across them and over the little plant Laura had brought in from the Plains.

"We should send these to your Uncle Arthur," she said. "See if he can't show them to someone at his school."

"Why? I thought you had broken off with him?" Laura glared across the table, her smile gone. Arthur, so like her father. He had a special place in Laura's heart. Only a year younger than Linwood, Arthur had made the trip out to meet the German who had replaced his brother and transplanted his nieces. It was inevitable that he and Hans would clash.

"Well, I haven't written since Hans threw him out and—well, you remember that day." Frances rubbed at the brown spots on her hands uncomfortably. "But he was very fond of you and Annabelle. He would be delighted to see these drawings."

"But what then?" Laura pressed. "He's so far away. What good would it do to send them to him? Besides, I like having them here." She blushed. "They make me feel—oh, I don't know … like I can retreat, if you understand. As though I can step away for awhile, be outside of things. Sometimes—I need that."

Oh, but Frances ached for her serious little girl, with her simple pleasures and secrets. She understood, of course. On some days, when the girls were milking or helping on the run, Frances liked nothing better than to sit at the piano—the same piano that Linwood had caressed and that had been dragged out here to this dry land—and wipe the keys with a damp cloth. That simple, unfussy motion, fingers tracing the yellow ivory, soothed her. Frances could not play a single tune, and neither could her girls—but just sitting at the keyboard brought memories into her body, of life before, with dear old Lin and their warm, tiny house balancing precariously on the pit-top. She remembered Linwood playing pieces before supper. Outside, on summer evenings, miners, in all their blackness, would stand and listen at the gate to the soft notes drifting through the open windows.

Their faces held the same, quiet look that Frances recognised on Sundays, when they listened to Linwood's sermon. Sometimes, when he played at night, they whistled, joining in. Then they carried on their way, and Lin and the girls would sit down to supper. These moments, relived at the piano in the arid, boiling air of the Plains, were refreshing. Frances embraced them, for they let her believe that life could carry on, that Hans meant well in all he did.

But, this morning, Frances knew she did not want this kind of in-spite-of happiness for her daughters. She did not want their lives to be one of compromise—let them build a kitchen with a whole wall of windows if they wanted. Let them spend their money on paints, and papers, and charcoals—but not red ribbon. And let them meet a husband who was not cruel, or persistent, or inconsiderate.

"Arthur may know something about a school or a scholarship," Frances said, speaking as the thoughts came to her. "You have such talent, Laura."

An odd thing happened to Laura's face. Emotions struggled for supremacy, and her mouth twisted up and down. She looked a little frightened but this was swiftly followed, Frances was sure, by a look of relief. "You would send me away?"

Frances felt a squeeze inside her ribs, and she hurriedly reached out to stroke her daughter's cheek. "Of course not!"

Laura shook her head. "There's no way Hans would allow it. He wouldn't let me go back to Father's family."

She was right. Hans controlled them. He barked rather than spoke; he prodded rather than caressed. Yet, Frances had to admit, to her deep shame, the arrogant way he held his body had been attractive in the early days. Labouring on a farm near to the pit, the guttural roll of his speech seemed exotic rather than alarming, so different from the flat vowels and mumbles of Linwood's parishioners. Hans bathed only once a week, so the odour of his toil, his physicality, followed him around like a cloud. It thrilled Frances in a way, she was sure, that Linwood would find wanton. Private moments with Linwood had always been awkward. With Hans, they were … rough but exhilarating. At least in the beginning.

He would not agree to Laura leaving. And she could see that her girl was now torn, tormented.

"Would this be something you could want, Laura?" she asked quietly.

The girl made the tiniest of nods. But she hesitated.

"Don't worry about me, or your sister," Frances said. "If I could swing it with Arthur for you to go home for a year or so, we would be fine here. Besides, it won't be long before Annabelle is your age, and she can help with all the baking and milking. Everything you do, she can do."

But this didn't seem to settle Laura at all, and Frances watched, bewildered, as her daughter started to clench and unclench her fists; little white lines appeared across her knuckles, thin bones pushing against pink skin. She was trembling.

"What is it?" Frances was bewildered. "It's not like you to take on so."

Very quietly: "I don't *want* Annabelle to do everything I do."

And then, with that tone and Laura's contorted control of her body, all other understandings of that morning, all realisations that Frances thought she had come to, were now deluged, drenched, swept away by a greater, sorrowful awareness. She understood—*fully* understood. Her heart seemed to rear backwards in her chest, pushing acidly against her spine. Those half-awake moments, when she thought Hans had slipped from their bed; the stains she had found in Laura's undergarments, which she had put down to natural growth—they were the phrases, the sentences of a darker language from which she had been excluded. And they were now translated for her, laid bare. A mesh, a veil had been lifted. Clarity, as stark as the blades of grass on Laura's painting, was reached.

How could I not have seen? Why were my eyes blind? And Frances impaled herself on these inward questions, hating, hating, hating herself. She reached across the table for her daughter, now aware of her own tears.

Laura allowed herself to be stroked and comforted for a while, the hair brushed back from her face by a mother's shaking fingertips. Then, slowly, she reached out for the plant brought in from the run, and turned it over in her fingers.

"What did you say?" Frances sniffed, wiping her face.

"I said, this is tutu." Laura held out the stalky green leaves and touched the red berries lightly. "Do you know anything about it?"

"Why?" Frances blinked rapidly. She wondered if Laura had been damaged some other way, if there had been some shift in her mind.

"Last spring I heard one of Sanderson's men say that the sheep had to be kept away from it. The berries are poisonous. If they eat just a little bit, their stomachs swell up and their intestines burst." Laura's voice was light and monotone.

Frances looked down at the plant. It sat placidly in Laura's palm, the berries glinting merrily in the sunlight. The leaves were feathered at the ends, tapered like a brush.

"A plant this size could kill a sheep, maybe two," Laura continued. She patted the leaves. "Aren't the berries a beautiful colour? So dark and red. Almost the colour of tea."

A sheep bleated on the run outside. Annabelle sang in the distance, probably in the shack, forcing sour milk into butter. Her thin arms had some strength, but not much, and she tired easily. Her tuneful melody floated into the kitchen through the open door and settled about the shoulders of the women, sitting mute and knowing. On the painting in front of them, three merino sheep chewed the grass contentedly, picking their way around a small green bush, studded with berries.

THE BEAST

Back home—his *real* home—it was not unknown for a man, when digging up chunks of peat, to discover an ancient, stony lava flow beneath. Even his father had done it, when prising earthy fudge from his land. A shovel might shatter or a pick-axe jar violently, shaking the unlucky man all the way up to his shoulder. And, lying patiently in the soil, was a grey seam of lava. No longer scarlet and searing—all of that had fizzled away thousands of years ago—but stubborn and defiantly present. And useful. Men forgot about the peat for the fire and hacked at the unexpected stone. Small outhouses or additional rooms were constructed and when fires were eventually lit, the hearth breathed new warmth into these old, never-forgetting rocks.

It was not unusual for Hans's thoughts to turn back to the cold lava of Mecklenberg when striding the boundary of the Sanderson run. The Canterbury Plains seemed to drive him backwards into his past, forcing him to compare the home of old and this new place. He felt the flats sneer at him as he searched for Sanderson's sheep. Bush fires might blacken them, January sun might scorch away their colour, but they were relentless. Not volcanic, not dramatic, but taut and set. Empty of the marshes and thickets that punctuated Mecklenberg's table-top land, the Plains gave up their spoils unwillingly. No hidden jewels beneath their surface, no rocks waiting to be bricked into homes. Instead, this part of New Zealand endured the tattooing of boundary markers, but reminded the settlers that they were insignificant with occasional flash floods, or snowstorms that swallowed flocks of sheep whole.

It was midday. Frances had packed bread and strips of cold mutton in his satchel, and Hans dropped it from his shoulder. He sat down on a small ridge, some distance from the boundary hut. One of Sanderson's men had left the hut in a bit of a state on his last trek to find sheep. Newspapers, tobacco on the floor. Hans tore at the bread. He would find out who it was and have words.

Having words. Hans grunted and swallowed. He'd had words this morning with Frances when she bleated on about knocking a hole in the kitchen wall and putting in a window. He'd had words with William Sanderson just last week when the man had not paid him again. Hans chewed his meat. Wages could be taken in other ways. There was, of course, plump, blinking, scared little Sarah Sanderson …

It would make things easier if William had taken off on the lurch. For Hans's favourite way of having words, lately, was with Sarah. Plump, blinking, scared little Sarah Sanderson. She knew, of course, what Hans's intentions were the first time William went to town. She must surely have read it in his face and the way he stared at her as he worked the fence around the homestead. But she had played coy and wept a little—silly girl. She was unlikely to tell anyone what had happened—what *was* happening—but better if William was not around to get suspicious. A little ball of worry bounced up in Hans's chest, and he pinched the flesh above his sternum, squeezing the anxiety away.

Calmer, he finished his meal and washed it down with cold tea, prising the cork from an old bottle with his teeth. No milk or sugar. Frances and her girls liked their tea pale and sweet, just as a baby would take it. Hans drank his straight from the pot. He kept some back in his bottle for later. Stalking errant sheep could be thirsty work.

Rubbing his hand over his face and bristles, Hans made to stand up. But something caught his eye, out in the brush. It was way off but it appeared to be crawling. Hans squinted and removed his hat, casting his face in shadow.

He waited. It wasn't a sheep, too big for that. And it was too far from the bush for it to be a boar.

And then, inexplicably, the round nub of panic in his chest that he thought he had rubbed away suddenly burst upwards, almost through his skin. It boiled in his throat. Hans slumped heavily on the earth. It was not an animal. He knew what it was.

§

Otto, Hans's grandfather, had been the first to see the Barghest. He told the family when they came back from milking. Hans was six, just old enough to help Father. He had walked into the little kitchen, hungry after an early morning, and there was Papa, his head in his hands, blanketed knees shaking next to the fire.

Over Hans's head, the adults held a whispered conversation. He half listened, keeping his head down and licking his bowl of lentils and bacon clean. Some words were said that he didn't understand, but he heard enough to realise that Papa had seen the black beast, the Barghest. Hans looked at his empty bowl. He was sad, for it meant that Papa would soon die.

As milk was warmed on the stove and passed around, Papa talked in his rough way. His legs had been particularly sore so he had lit the fire early. The stumps where shins and ankles used to be were always worse in the winter, he said, and some mornings he woke resentfully. Today, Papa went on, he hated his son and wife a little as they trooped past him to work the fields.

Grandmother had cried at this, and Father looked angry. Hans held his mother's skirt, bewildered. Later, as he lay at the end of his parents' bed and they thought Father was asleep, Mother explained that black thoughts invited the black beast. Soon after allowing those emotions to form, Papa had looked out the window into the corn and, crouched on its foul stomach, was a Barghest. Papa could do nothing to prevent what was coming.

"But if he had not looked out?" Hans asked.

His mother's eyes were bright in the darkness, and then Father's gruff voice cut through the night. "The Barghest would have shown itself another way, boy.

Now he has seen it, Papa has to say his farewells, for he has not long left with us."

Hans's mother sniffed.

"Enough, woman," Father barked. "The old man is weak. Better that the Barghest takes him before he starts asking for the doctor. Medical men cost money."

Hans reached out for his mother's foot beneath the bedclothes. "When I am big, I'm going to build a house with no windows. Or just one. That way I'll be safe from the beast when I'm at home."

Father snorted. "You're a fool, boy. Things happen because they are meant to happen. I was meant to find the lava that built this house, just as Papa was meant to see his death. Now sleep." His heel found Hans's ribs, prodding. "No snivelling tomorrow, only work."

§

The Barghest was still some way off. Hans was on all fours in the grass, straining to see. He daren't get up, knowing his legs would not hold him and that the beast would spot him. Hans quickly scanned the horizon. There was no one else about. The Barghest was for him alone.

His arms began to shake and he lay down in the dusty earth, stomach and chest placed flat on the sharp brush. He felt his heart pound, beating his fear into the earth. *Will this land sense my panic?* A little ribbon of thought passed through his mind. *If it does, it would surely not offer me succour. It must know I hate it as much as it hates me.*

He thought of his arrival, four years before, and the drift south to Christchurch. Frances and the girls in tow. Johanna had been so wrong, with her scratched words of hope. She might have made something out here, but her brother could not.

"It is easy to buy land," lied her letter. "Give up labouring, leave England. Don't return to Mecklenberg, there is only Father left. The meanness is still in him and you know how you argue. Come to New Zealand instead. My master has bought strips and strips of good farming land, and you can too."

Seven years younger than Hans, Johanna saw brightness in all things. She even believed Father's explanation for her mother's death—but she was wrong about the land. The best, most fertile was gone or too expensive. Frances had nothing to offer, for the fool Linwood gave away more than he took in wages. Hans had burned upon making that discovery. He had relied upon Linwood's widow sitting on a respectable pension, but the sale of her beaten down furniture barely covered the cost of the crossing.

After two years though, William Sanderson appeared at the Nelson woollen mill on business. He liked the sparseness of Hans's speech. Hans had learnt long ago that the fewer the words the better the impact, and Sanderson was drawn towards the German's silence like a magnet. A job on the Sanderson run was his if Hans wanted it. But Hans should have anticipated the resentment that came as he toiled another man's property. To own land was to be a man; to work a land not yours was to be little more than a serf.

There was a noise out on the flats and Hans raised his head. The beast had moved closer and he could make out its wiry fur. Hans held his breath, unwilling to give out the essence of himself in case the Barghest might smell him, and identify him. He thought of Papa, with his two stumps. At least Hans could run.

§

The house in Mecklenberg had turned itself inside out like a canker; plates and cups were not where they were supposed to be, soiled bedding lay in piles on an unswept floor instead of in the soak. Half-eaten food spilled from the mantelpiece. Johanna scurried from pot to fire, but her eight-year-old legs were not deft enough to boil the broth without burning the bread. She grinned though, when Hans and their father walked through the door, proud to feed them.

Father ate in silence, glancing at the empty seats beside the fire. The arms of Papa's chair were still stained with his sweat. Grandmother's glazed jugs sat on the mantelpiece, now dusty and chipped. Johanna glanced up at the brown pots and bit her lip.

"I broke one of Mama's jugs today, Father," she said. "I was trying to make a custard and it fell."

Father's reaction was swift. He reached across the table and cuffed the girl, slapping her head into her bowl. Hans, bread at his lips, paused. Then he ate, tucking himself out of the line of fire.

Johanna sat back, soup dripping from her hair. "I'm

sorry. But it was cracked and old—I didn't think …"

"I won't waste eggs on childish things," Father barked. "Your fool mother was too soft with you."

Johanna sank into herself. Her hands dropped onto her stained apron and twisted together, like dying birds. Broth dripped down her nose. Hans watched, swallowing his husk of bread and thin soup. He knew his father cared little for the trinkets his parents had left behind. But the farm was dying. Eggs could not be used on puddings, for these were hungry days.

Johanna's arms irritated him. They were too frail and thin to hold the scars and burns from cooking and baking. Did she think it was a game, this life? Making a custard, of all things. Hans leaned forward and pinched the flesh above Johanna's elbow. His fingers left pink marks.

"Do you hear our father?" he snapped.

Johanna's eyes were wet and her soft mouth fell open. Her hand drifted to her sore flesh. Hans could see her confusion. She used to make custards with Mother, before the woman's fall down the stairs took her child away from the safety of pencils and spinning tops, and pushed her into the kitchen and scullery.

"Johanna?" Hans leaned forward again, his fingers poised.

"Yes!" Johanna's voice was high. She sat rigidly in her seat.

Outside a neighbour shouted and a horse neighed. A cart was being loaded; there were jobs to be had in England. Hans laid down his spoon, aware his father was watching him. He looked out the window at his neighbour's smiling face, and then back to his sister's taut frame.

§

Papa had died three days after seeing the Barghest. Hans remembered his death distinctly. The old man had taken a fever and the breath boiled in his lungs. They could hear him at night, sitting in his chair beside the fire. He bubbled and frothed, and then died. By the time Grandmother came down in the morning, Papa was as stiff as a tree. Hans had hidden behind his mother as Father cracked the old man's fingers from the armchair, and hoisted the ancient bones over his shoulder.

So, now he had seen it, Hans could expect to have three days left. It seemed that was the way it went. But maybe the Barghest had to see *him*, for the two to be connected. Maybe if he slithered home on his belly, back to Frances, the beast would claim another.

But, in a tiny piece of his heart, Hans knew such an idea was folly. The Barghest appeared to those who had lived blackly, with foulness. Papa had hated the breath that gave him life, when he could no longer work. Perhaps the Beast had come for Father too, who could say? Hans had heard nothing from the man for ten years.

And what of Hans's own life? It was tarred with wrongdoing. A seam of badness was trapped beneath his skin. Back in England, around the mines and farms, he had been known as a dangerous man. Friday nights in the bar usually ended in a brawl, or a rough thrust with a woman, whether she wanted it or not. He had learned to take what he wanted and seek out distractions from a hard life where he could. Frances, Sarah, Laura, nameless others. The Barghest would not have to bite too deeply to taste the sourness at Hans's centre.

"Then I want it to be quick," he muttered and, without another thought, he stood up. The heat wrapped around him and he heard the crackle of dry grass. Hans held out his arms. "Come on! Do what you will!"

The beast snuffled, and the sound carried in the warm air. Hans licked his lips, swallowing the Barghest's rottenness. "I will fight you though! I will fight you to the death!"

The Barghest crept closer, claws scraping the scuffed earth. Black hair sprang upwards in tight curls. It glared at the man, standing on the ridge. Hans glared right back, squinting through the Canterbury sun.

Balance

by Shelly Davies

Haimona stood at the open doorway to the Sanderson homestead. He watched as the woman fluttered around her husband, offering him food and drink. She circled, sometimes reaching towards the man but never making contact. She tried, unsuccessfully, to keep her wide-eyed gaze away from both her husband's black eye and the Māori in the doorway.

Haimona considered taking a step over the doorsill and imagined what the pathetic white man would do about it. Or rather, not do. Haimona could hardly believe how much these English were constrained by their ideas of what was "proper". Sanderson's unwillingness to cross those thresholds of propriety allowed Haimona to impose himself on the man, back at the guesthouse—to insist he travel with him—and to stand here, right now. If any man marked Haimona's face he would not live for long, let alone enter the *pā* as an invited guest.

But he remained standing on the doorstep, watching. He knew that Sanderson could pretend nothing had happened on the plains because no one had been there to witness it. But to step into the house, with his wife there to see, and the keen eyes of the farmhands never far away: *that* would force even this insipid man to respond. It didn't matter what colour their skin—all men had fragile egos. Himself included.

Haimona watched Sanderson bat his wife away, the man's nose in the air even as he sat to remove his muddy boots. Sanderson had his back to the door. Haimona knew this was intended to offend, to emphasise Haimona's insignificance. Instead, though, the Māori saw it as a sign of weakness. Vulnerability. A wise and a strong man would never turn his back on a potential enemy. Haimona scoffed inwardly. How could this man protect a wife and family? If he could expose himself to danger so easily, what else might be going on under his nose?

Haimona breathed deeply, slowly, and settled his feet into a comfortable stance. Possibly Sanderson thought if he was left standing there long enough he would leave. But the white man was wrong. He wasn't going anywhere.

The woman busied herself with preparing food, a pie of some kind that smelled good and made Haimona's mouth water. Her dress clung tight around her middle, her stomach shaped like an egg. He watched her nibble anxiously as she worked. A piece of pie crust here, a slice of fruit there.

She laid a table with a cloth, fine china and silverware. The white man's habits were strange and misguided in so many ways, but they had something Haimona wanted: luxury. Comfort. He looked around the farmhouse, with its white walls and cushioned chairs. Polished furniture. It was worlds apart from *pā* life with dirt floors and raupo huts. He would have a house like this for his family. He would work and trade and travel until he did. White men would not turn their backs on him when he had a house like this.

When the table was set for one and a piping cup of hot tea was placed beside the plate, the woman cleared her throat timidly.

"William." She glanced at Haimona in the doorway.

Sanderson followed her gaze and harrumphed. "Get Hans. Tell him to put the man in the shearers' quarters."

Haimona watched colour drain rapidly from the woman's face. She didn't move.

"Go on," Sanderson said.

§

Haimona could barely believe how Hans stared at Sanderson's wife as she walked back into the homestead. He would kill a man who looked at Aotea that way. And Sanderson hadn't even looked up from his plate as Hans walked into the kitchen and helped himself to a piece of pie. Did this Hans have complete run of the farm? With Sanderson travelling so much it appeared so. But Haimona wouldn't trust Hans with anything. He seemed a man of few words, sharp edged. He had a bad *wairua* about him.

Haimona didn't know if he would ever understand these white men. They had no honour. No *mana*.

§

The bed came at the cost of work, but Haimona wouldn't have had it any other way. To be in another's debt brought things out of balance, and that didn't sit well with Māori. It was clear that Sanderson was in debt to Hans—well behind on the stockman's wages, Hans announced loudly and often. Didn't Sanderson see that the longer Hans wasn't paid the more power he had over his employer? Balance, *utu*, *tapu* and *noa*—ensuring and restoring equilibrium was a powerful principle these white men seemed to know nothing about.

Mustering time, and Haimona was an extra pair of hands. Days of it, separating ewes, rams, wethers. He refused to crutch sheep, though—he was cleaning sheep shit for no man. But the other work, the picking out of sheep—that he could do. Maybe he would trade for some sheep to take home. The meat was good, the animals easy to care for. He thought of Aotea in the kitchen of his fine white man's house, cooking mutton for their *whānau*. He liked that idea.

After a fortnight Haimona had settled into the daily routine. A wash in the icy creek and *karakia* to set the day right—two acts he was sure the man Hans rarely performed, for he stank to high heaven. And the only time he seemed to speak to any gods, Christian or otherwise, was to curse them loudly for his misfortunes. Which ranged from an uncooperative ewe to a burr in his boot, and apparently every single item of food or drink he ever put into his mouth.

Hans had a wife who appeared daily to cook the white men breakfast. Hans seemed to make her skittish—the tea was too bitter, bread too dry, porridge too salty. Haimona knew men from home who complained like Hans—men who raised themselves by keeping others down. Weak men, all of them sharing certain characteristics, regardless of where they came from, or whatever language they spoke—pride, fear, and a sharp tongue to try to hide it.

A day at the muster, and Hans swore at a ram that kicked him when he flipped it to shear off the heavy dags. Haimona saw darkness behind the white man's eyes: it didn't seem to be the paint of mud and the long, cold hours of working the land. Sadness, maybe, he thought. But, more likely, something else.

They stopped for lunch and a figure crossed the paddock towards the yards. Laura, the girl Haimona thought was Hans's stepdaughter. She was pretty, a woman in body, but walked with her head low and barely spoke. She carried a basket covered with a cloth.

"Mother sent me with lunch," she mumbled, clearly to Hans. A glance at Haimona.

"What?" Hans scowled. "Speak up girl!"

Swallowed words, barely audible. Haimona strained to hear.

"Lunch," Laura said again. She stood with the basket in front of her, arms wrapped around it.

Hans glowered at her. He sighed deeply and let go of the ram with a shove and an unnecessary boot up the arse to send it on its way. "Give it then." He climbed over the rails and walked towards her.

Laura held the basket out towards him, her arms outstretched. Haimona watched her turn her head away slightly. She flinched, her body pulling into itself as Hans snatched the basket from her hands. He saw relief on her face when Hans dismissed her. "Go on then."

§

That night, as Haimona drifted to sleep in the shearers' quarters, his thoughts were of his ancestors, the gods. *Atua*.

Tāne, god of the forest, brought his brothers into *Te Ao Marama*, the World of Light, by separating their parents. He forced the lovers apart, breaking their unyielding embrace, which until that time had kept their children in darkness. In the world with his brothers he soon recognised an imbalance. And so he reached down into the red earth of *Papatūānuku*, his mother, and breathed life into *Hine-Ahu-One*, the first woman.

Since that time his people had valued and treasured women, the *whare tangata* or house of man. There had to be balance. Without woman there was no man. And so, for Māori, even though it was the men who were out the front in the war parties, politicking and making speeches, women were a powerful influence. A force to be reckoned with. A wise man made sure he had women on his side, at his back, in his bed. There was strength in that—in recognising and protecting the *mana* of women.

From what little he knew of the white man's world, this was yet another thing they got wrong. Their women were powerless. But imbalance always demands to be put right.

§

Fence mending took Haimona over near the stockman's house. He watched how the cottage changed when Hans was gone. From a dank, clouded-over place that echoed with the voice of ghosts, to a place where sunrays sometimes bounced off the tin roof and the voice of a loving mother carried out into the yard. Giggling daughters, warming his ears. He thought of Aotea and his *whānau*. He had been gone too long. It was time to go home. But.

Laura was sitting in the shade of a *puriri* tree not far from the cottage. She had positioned herself so that if a horse were to cross the paddock she would hear it coming, but she'd be hidden from the rider's view. Haimona had noticed her do this most days, working something in her hands and often looking up to scan her surroundings. One time when she heard the hoof beats of Hans returning, she scrambled up and hid her treasure in the tree.

White women were scarce on the Plains, but this girl had something especially rare in her. Something the English propriety and her abrasive stepfather hadn't been able to quash. Every day she sat and held something in her hands; something Hans would not approve of. She was the one, Haimona had decided, to help restore balance.

When she got up from the tree, tucking her special things under her apron, Haimona called quietly out to her.

"*E kōtiro*," he said. "Girl."

She stopped walking and looked at him.

He pointed to a small bush nearby. "Do you know what this plant is?"

Publishing Credits

Versions of these stories have appeared in the following:

"A Pickled Egg"

> – *The London Magazine*, Aug/Sep 2008

"Mr William Sanderson Strikes for Home"

> – *The New Storyteller*, May 2009,
> www.newstoryteller.com/mrwilliamsanderson-
> strikesforhome.html

> – *First Steps Press*, July 2010,
> www.fspressonline.org/SSM/mr-william-sanderson-
> strikes-for-home/

"Miss Swainson's Girl"

> – *Random Acts of Writing*, July 2009

"Dottie"

> – *Halfway Down the Stairs*, Sept 2009,
> www.halfwaydownthestairs.net/index.php?action=
> view&id=133

The Authors

Rebecca Burns is an award-winning writer of short stories, over thirty of which have been published online or in print. She was nominated for a Pushcart Prize in 2011, winner of the Fowey Festival of Words and Music Short Story Competition in 2013 (and runner-up in 2014), and has been profiled as part of the University of Leicester's "Grassroutes Project"—a project that showcases the 50 best transcultural writers in the county.

The Settling Earth is her second collection of short stories. Her debut collection, *Catching the Barramundi,* was published in 2012—also by Odyssey Books—and was longlisted for the Edge Hill Award in 2013.

You can read more about Rebecca at
www.rebecca-burns.co.uk

Shelly Davies is of the Ngātiwai tribe. She's been publishing short stories, poetry, and academic work internationally for almost 20 years. She has edited two collections of indigenous writing: *Waiataata* and *Waiataata: Te Ata Hāpara.* She's a mother of three and is soon to become a grandmother for the first time—a fact she's still trying to wrap her head around!

Lightning Source UK Ltd.
Milton Keynes UK
UKOW04f0918090315

247545UK00001B/11/P